FLiRT

Copycat

By Nicole Clarke

GROSSET & DUNLAP
Published by the Penguin Group
Penguin Group (USA) Inc., 375 Hudson Street,
New York, New York 10014, U.S.A.
Penguin Group (Canada), 90 Eglinton Avenue East, Suite
700, Toronto, Ontario, Canada M4P 2Y3
(a division of Pearson Penguin Canada Inc.)
Penguin Books Ltd, 80 Strand, London WC2R 0RL, England
Penguin Ireland, 25 St Stephen's Green, Dublin 2, Ireland
(a division of Penguin Books Ltd)
Penguin Group (Australia), 250 Camberwell Road,
Camberwell, Victoria 3124, Australia
(a division of Pearson Australia Group Pty Ltd)
Penguin Books India Pvt Ltd, 11 Community Centre,
Panchsheel Park, New Delhi - 110 017, India
Penguin Group (NZ), Cnr Airborne and Rosedale Roads,
Albany, Auckland 1311, New Zealand
(a division of Pearson New Zealand Ltd)
Penguin Books (South Africa) (Pty) Ltd, 24 Sturdee
Avenue, Rosebank, Johannesburg 2196, South Africa

Penguin Books Ltd, Registered Offices:
80 Strand, London WC2R 0RL, England

Copyright © 2007 by Grosset & Dunlap. All rights reserved. Published by Grosset & Dunlap, a division of Penguin Young Readers Group, 345 Hudson Street, New York, New York 10014. GROSSET & DUNLAP is a trademark of Penguin Group (USA) Inc. Printed in the U.S.A.

Library of Congress Cataloging-in-Publication Data is available.

ISBN 978-0-448-44561-8   10 9 8 7 6 5 4 3 2 1

FLiRT
Copycat

By Nicole Clarke

Grosset & Dunlap

stalkerazzi.com

Currently stalking . . . former child star Georgia Cooper . . . spotted in Times Square yammering on her Juicy Couture Sidekick and carrying—what else?—the latest Chanel handbag. A top secret Stalkerazzi informant revealed to us first that Georgia's now one of Josephine Bishop's summer lackeys (you may have heard them called "interns") for the utterly divine fashion magazine *Flirt*. Keep your eyes peeled, faithful stalkers, for Georgia sightings this summer—we'll post 'em here! And Georgie Girl, since we know you're reading this, welcome to NYC!

Now fetch us a latte, will ya?

The celebrity gossip blogs weren't lying: Georgia Cooper turned the corner of 42nd Street and Broadway and headed straight for the glass-and-chrome tower of the Hudson-Bennett building. *Flirt*, Georgia's most favorite glossy on the planet, was located on the top floor. She had big plans for the summer: write a few knock-your-socks-off features, turn a few heads, and change a few minds about what a Hollywood ingenue can do once handed a pen. So her Hollywood career was stagnating—ahem—a little, so what! She had a new career in mind. This was her chance.

Georgia reached the revolving glass doors and braced herself. She knew she was about to be bombarded by fans who'd probably been waiting in the lobby since the building opened. How could they not be waiting, now that her job at *Flirt* was all over the Web? She had scads of fans.

Anyone who'd owned a TV in the last decade had seen *Molly Mack*, the sitcom that had made Georgia famous. She'd played the title role of the girl detective from the time she was seven until she turned eleven. Then the show got canceled. But five years later, with the show in eternal syndication, Georgia was still recognized everywhere she went. Her trademark flame red hair—the bangs, the long waves past her shoulders—gave her away. She still had her freckles, too. Plus, it wasn't like she discouraged the attention. Far from it. If someone called her name on the street, she'd turn and pose for the photo op, not hide her face in her jacket and run away. (Unlike *some* people Georgia wouldn't mention.)

So Georgia prepped for that first moment of recognition. She put on a wide, gracious smile, showing all her teeth. She kept her sunglasses on—she never went outside without them—to give herself that alluring air of mystery. She pushed through the revolving glass door and stepped into the lobby to find . . .

No fans.

No autograph hounds.

Not even a security guard stealing a shot on his camera phone.

Maybe my fans got the address wrong, she thought. *Maybe everyone thinks I start next week.*

And did I say I even care? Because I don't. I'm not in the mood for flashbulbs in my face right now, anyway. It's way too early.

She crossed the lobby and approached the security desk to sign in. The guard made her show ID, but upon seeing it his expression didn't change. There was her name on her ID—Georgia Cooper, yes, *the* Georgia Cooper from TV—and he acted like she was a random no one from, oh, who knows, Idaho.

"Sign here," he said. Georgia realized it was the guest log for the building, not a sheet of paper for his "niece."

She did her usual signature with the flourish under the second *g*. "Now don't go selling that," she teased him with a wink (a Molly Mack trademark), but he just gazed back at her like she'd told him not to eat soap.

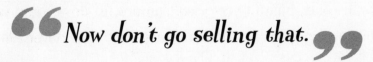
" Now don't go selling that. "

"Ooo-kay," he said and handed her a garish *GUEST* sticker that she was expected to attach to her shirt. "Go on through," he told her, pointing to the electronic turnstile that was the final obstacle before the elevators.

Georgia was shocked. And she was shocked further when a small group of office workers pushed past her without a second glance. They took over an entire elevator and let the doors close before she could squeeze in. Did these people not realize whose toe they'd almost stepped on?

New Yorkers, Georgia thought. *They're so jaded.*

This complete and total nonrecognition wasn't helping her nerves. Just imagine: You're "it" one minute, "not it" the next. She'd need time to adapt. Back in Hollywood, she'd been chased by rabid fans through Grauman's Chinese Theatre (okay, it was a group of junior-high girls, and they may have confused her with Lindsay Lohan). She'd had paparazzi stake out her driveway in the Hollywood Hills to see what kind of sweatpants she wore to check the mailbox. She'd even been asked for her autograph while at the doctor's for strep throat. And this wasn't all because she'd briefly dated Anton Stone, the actor inches from the A-list—because they had broken up over three months ago and everyone still knew her name.

Georgia checked her hair in the mirrored wall as she waited for another elevator. She looked presentable. Good, because her hairdresser wasn't around to do a touch-up. This low-key lifestyle was like immersing herself in regular

> **66** *This complete and total nonrecognition wasn't helping her nerves.* **99**

life for some movie role. Not that she'd ever *had* a movie role, but she'd heard that's what serious actors did when they did movies. This summer she'd do her own hair, prep her own meals, and get used to *not* signing her name on every available surface. She was Georgia Cooper, simple intern, from . . . it may as well have been Idaho. She only wished she had some lines to memorize so she'd know what to say.

A girl standing nearby interrupted her thoughts. "This elevator's free," she called.

The girl wheeled a small, neat suitcase into the elevator. She was about Georgia's age, with sleek honey blond hair to her shoulders and bangs, too, although hers were cowlick-free. (Even Georgia's Hollywood-trained hairdresser couldn't get her bangs to lay flat in that one spot.) The elevator girl also had perfect skin, a perfect nose, and large, long-lashed blue eyes that she was clearly trying to show off by not wearing sunglasses. But she wore the *GUEST* badge stuck to the front of her preppy shirt, so she didn't belong there, either.

"Excuse me . . . I don't mean to be rude, but are you—" the girl started, and here Georgia's heart lifted. But they were interrupted by a twenty-something woman who shoved herself into the elevator before the doors closed.

The woman let out a little gasp. "I recognize you!" she burst out.

Georgia opened her mouth, about to say that yes, she'd do an autograph, sure, but the woman was talking to the elevator girl instead.

"I saw your photo in *Publishers Weekly*. You're the one Constance Gack just signed, am I right? Elizabeth . . . Cheekwood?"

Georgia closed her mouth.

The elevator girl—Elizabeth—blushed a pleasant shade of pale pink and admitted that she was Elizabeth Cheekwood. "I can't believe Constance signed me," she gushed. "I know I'm young to get a literary agent, and such an important one . . . I guess I'm just really lucky." She had a very faint Southern accent and was being ever-so-polite. Georgia had to hold back her gag reflex.

"Oh, it's not luck," said the woman. "Obviously you're a very talented writer. Constance Gack wouldn't have signed you otherwise."

"No," Elizabeth said, smiling. "Really, it's just luck."

The woman laughed. Elizabeth laughed. Georgia did not laugh.

The elevator stopped at the woman's floor, but she held the door open and turned to Georgia. "Constance Gack is one of the most prestigious literary agents in the country," she explained. "And she signed Elizabeth here based on just the first few chapters of her novel. It's incredible. And Elizabeth is only—how old are you, Elizabeth?"

"Sixteen," she said, her cheeks doing that whole rosy charade.

Sixteen! Georgia was sixteen. And all she'd finished writing so far in her measly life was the application essay that got her the *Flirt* internship. She'd started writing some other things, but she'd lost momentum after about page two. Probably because she'd had no one to show them to. Her aforementioned hairdresser didn't read anything without pictures.

"Hmm," Georgia said without further comment.

"Well, congratulations, Elizabeth," the woman said. "I look forward to buying your book one day." She let the doors close.

Now Elizabeth and Georgia were alone together, heading up to the top floor. Elizabeth was also going to *Flirt*.

Don't tell me the prodigy is also an intern, Georgia thought. Instead she said lightly, "A novel, huh?"

"Yeah. But it's not like I've written the whole thing yet," Elizabeth said, shrugging. "She made it out to be so much more than it is."

Sweet act, Georgia thought. *Guess what? I'm not buying it.*

She was Not Happy. Was it not enough that she was a TV star? Now she had to be a novelist, too? All she'd wanted from this summer was the chance to try writing. Now she felt like a late bloomer and, worse, like a fake. If this was what the other interns were like, she was toast.

Might as well head back for the Hills.

The elevator doors opened at their floor and they both stepped out. Elizabeth touched her elbow. "I thought she was talking to you at first," she said in a low voice. "Aren't you Molly Mack?"

Georgia sighed. "Yes, but today I'm just an intern."

"You too? This is unbelievable. I'm an intern, too! My name's—"

"I know, I heard," Georgia cut in. "Elizabeth Cheekwood, literary sensation."

"You can call me Lizzy," she said. "That's what my friends at school call me."

"You can call me Georgia," Georgia said. No way were they going to be friends.

"Georgia, I love your show. That one where you found the lost puppy? And that one where you got the crank phone calls? I thought you were here to be interviewed, you know, *for* the magazine. Not work at it."

Georgia sniffed. Her usual

> **66 Yes, but today I'm just an intern. 99**

enthusiasm when faced with her fans was squashed under the weight of Elizabeth's book contract. "We need to sign in," Georgia said. She headed for the reception desk and Elizabeth followed.

Before they reached the reception desk, a grim-looking woman emerged from an opaque glass doorway. She was twenty-five, tops, but she dressed decades older, like a kid playing dress-up in Mommy's office clothes. Her dark red hair was tightly wound into a pointy knot. Georgia—a natural redhead who had a knack for spotting the fakers—knew straight off that the color was from a bottle. The woman wore a tiny headset at her ear, as if she couldn't spend a single second away from her phone console.

"Welcome to *Flirt*," the woman said. "I know you're Georgia"—she said it without a hint of excitement—"and I assume you're Elizabeth. I'm Delia Zelman, Ms. Bishop's *personal* assistant."

The way she said "personal" made Georgia almost laugh out loud. Elizabeth, however, seemed impressed.

Delia led them through the glass door. "You are the first two interns to arrive," she said. She started marching down a hallway, and Georgia and Elizabeth hurried to keep up. Delia talked as she walked. "We're doing the intern orientation differently this year. Meaning there isn't time for an official orientation because we're scrambling to close a big issue. So instead, we've arranged for you to meet with Ms. Bishop and the department heads at ten." She stopped.

Georgia took a breath and looked around. They were in a wide, open room that seemed to take up the entire floor. In the far distance were giant windows that showed off a view of Times Square, the central hub of Manhattan. But between those giant windows and where Georgia, Elizabeth, and Delia stood were a series of small compartments surrounded by low, muted gray walls. Cubicles. They were like open-air closets, or low-security prison cells. And they went on and on—cubicle after cubicle after cubicle. Georgia felt like she'd stepped onto the wrong show's set on the soundstage. When she'd imagined the offices of *Flirt* magazine, she'd thought Glamour. She'd thought Elegance. She did not think Gray Hive of Cubicles.

"This," Delia said, "is your cube, Georgia." She indicated a nearby compartment. "Go settle in. Find a place to stow your things." She gave Georgia a once-over.

Georgia stood up straight, knowing she'd pass inspection. She had to. When getting ready for this day, she'd thought of it like a new role. She was playing "Magazine Intern" for the next two months, and in order to get into character, she made sure to dress for the part. She'd determined her wardrobe straight from the pages of the magazine. Her first-day-on-the-job outfit included a skirt and shirt by Dior, shoes by Chloé, and sunglasses by

Marc Jacobs. She had *Flirt* written all over her. Any casting director—or magazine editor—could see that.

Delia gave a curt nod. Georgia knew she'd passed.

"Don't you have a suitcase?" Delia asked.

"Oh, my driver has my bags. He'll have them delivered to the loft today."

"Your driver?" Delia said, raising a dark red eyebrow. *Did she dye those, too?* Georgia thought, grudgingly impressed at the effort.

"My driver came with me from LA," Georgia explained. "Of course, I'm going to send him home. I don't need a driver this summer."

"Good," Delia said. "Because you'd be the first intern to have a personal driver while here."

Delia handed Georgia a glossy black binder and gave another to Elizabeth. The *Flirt* logo was emblazoned on the cover in crimson.

"You'll see from the tag inside your binder what your assignment is and who your mentor will be," Delia said. "Now, Georgia, be sure to be in Room 399B at ten A.M. sharp. Elizabeth, follow me. I'll show you to your cube."

Georgia opened her binder. The tag inside said

❝My driver came with me from LA. Of course, I'm going to send him home. I don't need a driver this summer.❞

Department: Entertainment—score!—but listed under *Mentor* was nothing. Just an empty space.

As in I have no mentor? Georgia thought.

"Wait!" Georgia called out, and Delia paused mid-march. "What do you mean, mentor?"

"Mine's Josephine Bishop," Elizabeth said, with a glance at Delia.

Delia nodded approvingly. "Features is a choice position. The opportunity to work so closely with Ms. Bishop is exceptional."

Georgia's stomach sank a little at that—wasn't the Features internship the only writing slot?—but she had a more important question for Delia. "Where's my mentor? It's blank."

"Ms. Bishop will explain everything," Delia said dismissively. Then she held up a finger, listening to her headset. "That's security," she said. "Another batch of interns has arrived. Elizabeth, let me show you to your cube and then I'll go out to greet them."

"I can find it," Elizabeth said quickly. "You don't need to show me."

"Fine," Delia said, clearly unconcerned. "Your cube is just over there, against the window. You'll see the nameplate." She left for the reception area.

When she was gone, Georgia set her Chanel bag on her desk and took in her "cube," as Delia had called it. The nameplate on the gray half wall surrounding her desk said

Georgia Cooper. It was official. This was *her* desk. She'd never before had a job outside a TV studio, so technically this might be considered her first real job, ever. She sat in *her* swivel chair. She kicked off and started to spin.

And when she spun in the direction of the corridor, Elizabeth was still there.

"Elizabeth, shouldn't you go find your desk?"

"Georgia, please call me Lizzy." She entered Georgia's cubicle space. With just one other person in there, Georgia realized that the cubicle was about a quarter of the size of her trailer from her last acting job, the all-in-one shampoo/conditioner commercial. A quarter of the size of a shampoo spot's trailer! That was small.

"This is so exciting," Elizabeth said. "Two whole months on our own in New York City—it's like the best summer vacation ever."

"I don't know about that," Georgia said. "First off, I don't think we'll be on our own. We're supposed to live with a housemother. And two? I doubt it'll be a vacation."

Elizabeth was acting like this was all so *easy*. It wasn't easy for Georgia. She'd worked hard to get a shot at this internship, and she expected to work hard this summer to prove herself.

Besides, she'd just been on vacation—to Cabo. Now it was time to get serious.

"Oooh, turn on your computer," Elizabeth said,

shifting gears. "Let's go online and check out the clubs. Aren't you dying to go to a club tonight?"

Georgia shrugged. In truth, she'd already made appearances at three of the hottest clubs just the previous night. Even if she went to a club or two that night, no way was she letting a wide-eyed tourist tag along.

Elizabeth was hopping up and down in excitement. "I bet you know the exact right places to go tonight, don't you?" she said.

"Just beautiful," Georgia said. "This is your first time in New York, isn't it?"

"I've been to New York before," Elizabeth said defensively. "With my mom. She's a lobbyist—we live in Virginia, you know, just outside D.C. But she's always coming up to New York for work stuff. She let me come with her a couple times. She took me to the Met, and to MoMA. We saw *Les Mis* on Broadway. It was annoying, though, because she never let me go out by myself. So this summer—let's just say I have a list of everything I want to do." She leaned close to Georgia and confided, "It's a long list."

Georgia swiveled her chair away from Elizabeth. In mere minutes they would meet the head of a magazine empire and all Elizabeth could think about was club hopping. *I guess once you get a book deal with a megafancy literary agent, you don't have a care in the world,* she thought. "Whatever," she said aloud.

Elizabeth reached out and hit the power button on

Georgia's computer. A cartoon animation popped up on the screen instead of a normal login window. There was an oddly dressed, pigtailed cartoon character staring back at them, enormous eyes blinking at lightning speed. It looked like something from a Japanese anime movie.

A speech balloon said: **Good luck, newbie intern! You'll need it, lad. Muwahahahahahaha.**

"That's weird," Elizabeth said.

Georgia tried hitting a key, any key. The animation didn't stop. *Is this how the magazine greets its new interns?* she thought.

"It's stuck?" Elizabeth said. "You can't get to the Internet? I've got to drop off my suitcase, anyway—let's use my computer." She wheeled her suitcase out of the cubicle, then stopped in the corridor. "Aren't you coming?"

"Does it look like I'm coming?" Georgia asked. She hadn't moved a muscle.

"No . . ." Elizabeth said. But still she hovered, waiting for Georgia to get up.

Georgia leaned back in her chair, clearly not going anywhere. "That's because I'm not coming," she said. "You're slow on the uptake, aren't you?"

Elizabeth blinked. "Um, okay," she said unsteadily. "So I guess I'll see you in that room at ten, then."

"Sure thing," Georgia said sweetly. Then she turned back to her computer so she could make that gigantic pigtailed head stop its interminable bouncing.

ⓖ   ⓖ   ⓖ   ⓖ

Ten A.M., Room 399B, and if this were a TV show, Georgia would have it cast already. There was the good girl, Elizabeth, although audiences would soon discover she wasn't *that* good. There was the rebel, this one with blue tips dyed in her hair. There was the basket case: She came in last, saying she'd gotten lost. The artist had long, wild hair and wore every color she could get her hands on with the nuisance of proper matching. The shy one didn't speak unless spoken to. The overachiever already had her pen poised to take notes.

And who was left? The star, of course. She starts the show completely misunderstood, but—just one episode in—you'll fall head over heels for her.

Or so Georgia hoped. She sat at the long table in the conference room with the other six interns, waiting for the important people to arrive. The editors filed in one or two at a time, looking harried. Finally, a glamorous woman walked in and took a seat at the head of the table. She had dark hair in a tight chignon, sharp cheekbones, and deftly painted lips. She wore a severe white suit and spike heels that could cut through glass. She had to be Josephine Bishop, the editor-in-chief.

❝ If this were a TV show, Georgia would have it cast already. ❞

The woman clapped her hands for attention and every girl—except Georgia, who had been studying her closely—jumped. "Girls," she began, "I'm Josephine Bishop, the founding editor of this magazine and the originator of this internship program." She spoke in a crisp, commanding voice that made Georgia sit up straighter. The other girls did the same. Ms. Bishop continued. "This internship is a reward, to be sure, but it's also an immense amount of work. More work than I'm sure many of you have ever done." Her eyes swept around the room, seeming to land on Georgia.

She's not looking at me. Wait, is *she looking at me?*

The magazine's editors murmured knowingly, as if the girls were about to be forced to scrub the shiny walls of the conference room with their travel toothbrushes.

Ms. Bishop's gaze moved to Elizabeth. "Know that you are each here due to your raw talent. I handpicked every one of you. And I have high expectations. So don't disappoint me."

Georgia listened, afraid to move.

"Now," Ms. Bishop continued, "let's get on with the introductions." She swept her arm around the table to identify each of the editors in quick succession: "Quinn Carson, Managing Editor. Gayle Bailor, Health and Fitness. Naomi Wu, Beauty. Demetria Tish, Fashion. Lynn Stein, Photography. Trey Narkisian, Co-Managing Editor, Electronic Content. And I trust you know that in addition to overseeing the staff, I also head up Features."

Georgia's head spun with all the names. Usually people knew her name and she didn't need to keep track of theirs.

However, Georgia did notice one very important thing: No editor was in the room to represent Entertainment, the department she was assigned to. So it was true what her binder said—she was mentorless.

Before Georgia could ask, Ms. Bishop beat her to it. "You'll notice there is someone missing. The Entertainment editor was recently let go." She met eyes with one of the editors—Georgia thought it was Quinn. "Not so recently, I'll admit," she continued. "We've had trouble filling the position, but I assure you we're nearing the end of our search. So"—and here her eyes landed on Georgia—"I imagine, Georgia, that you'd like to know what this means in terms of your mentor this summer."

"I *was* wondering," Georgia said. She felt everyone's eyes on her. The basket case—the girl with the messy bun across from her—seemed especially sympathetic.

"I'll be working with you myself. That is, until someone is hired." Georgia practically glowed. Talk about good fortune. The only downside would be having to share her mentor with Elizabeth, who, by the way, hadn't met eyes with Georgia since they'd entered the conference room.

Georgia felt a pang, realizing how nasty she must have sounded before.

Ah well. It's not like we're doing the buddy system here.

Ms. Bishop was now asking the girls to go around the room and introduce themselves. She turned to the shy intern first, a tall, gorgeous girl with cocoa skin and long skinny braids cascading down her shoulders. "I'm Nailah," she started. "Nailah Jansen."

She paused, and Ms. Bishop waved a hand for her to continue. She obviously had no patience for the meek.

"From Cape Town in South Africa," Nailah said. "This is my first visit to the States." She turned to her new supervisor, Gayle Bailor. "Health and Fitness is the exact internship I was hoping for. After I injured my knee"—a strained look hovered on her face, then vanished just as quickly—"I found a new focus in fitness. Eating healthy and working out are both very important to me. I would love to encourage *Flirt* readers to live healthy lifestyles." She clammed up then, looking down at her hands.

"I'm happy to have you, Nailah," Gayle said.

"Yes, happy," Ms. Bishop said quickly, as if impatient with such earnestness. She turned to the other interns. "You may remember the article we ran last year on international track stars—Nailah was one of the girls we featured. We're sorry to hear about your knee, Nailah, but we are lucky to have you in a different capacity."

Nailah smiled but didn't look up from her hands.

The girl next to Nailah started talking. "And I'm

Asha Patel, from Mumbai, India." Georgia watched the girl she'd pegged as the overachiever intently. She was pretty, with dark hair to her shoulders that was sort of curly, sort of not, and wore owl-eye glasses. She had a sharp, determined look in her dark eyes. She looked serious about being there, and *smart*. Not to prove Georgia wrong, Asha began explaining what she hoped to accomplish with her internship in the Beauty department. She had an interest in cosmetology, although, according to her parents, her knowledge of chemistry would only get her one step closer to becoming a doctor. Specifically, a surgeon.

Ms. Bishop waited, a stiff smile on her face. Asha's supervisor, Naomi Wu, also waited. A doctor was a profession any sixteen-year-old would be encouraged to aspire to—in any other room. But this was a fashion magazine, and why spend a summer here if all you wanted was to grow up and perform triple-bypass surgeries? The look on Asha's face made it clear that she knew how contradictory she sounded.

"That is what my *pitaji* and *mataji*, my father and mother, want for me. But"—and here her eyes lit up—"being at *Flirt* is my dream come true. Someday I would like to create my own makeup line." She turned to Naomi. "The feature in the last issue, about the makeup artists? It was my favorite piece."

Naomi seemed pleased. "That was a favorite of mine, as well. And Asha, I'm sure your parents will come around when they see how much you'll be learning this summer."

Asha didn't look too convinced. How awful for her to have such strict parents. Georgia could do whatever she wanted and her mom went along with it—oh, it didn't hurt that Georgia had bought her mom her last two cars and whatever else she needed. As for her dad, he wasn't around and hadn't been since Georgia was four years old. It was better that way, Georgia told herself—one less person she had to listen to.

Next came the girl who'd walked in late: Sivya Levy, from Tel Aviv, Israel. She had family in Brooklyn, she said, so she'd been to New York before. She had curly, pale brown hair that was held in a bun with a rubber band, and not a single item of jewelry, not one. She glanced around at the other interns and then indicated her own simple outfit—a black T-shirt that said "I ♡ Geeks" and black cargo pants. She was also wearing *sneakers*, like she was going skateboarding! "I guess it's clear I'm not here for my fashion sense," Sivya joked.

Ms. Bishop gave a slight, almost imperceptible nod. It didn't seem mean, but it was clear from the way her eyes settled on Sivya's cheap, silk-screened T-shirt that she wasn't exactly pleased with the intern's chosen ensemble.

Sivya didn't appear to notice. She continued. "So, yeah, one of my hobbies is learning new languages—and by that I mean computer languages, not ancient Greek—

just last week I had a breakthrough with Perl." She had on a self-deprecating grin, but she was obviously proud of this "Perl" knowledge, whatever that was. Georgia guessed it had nothing to do with oysters.

Trey, the head of Electronic Content, looked excited about this Perl confession. "How are you with Java?" he asked, his eyes actually twinkling.

"So good you'll be buying me presents."

"Is that so?" Trey teased.

"I like dark chocolate," Sivya said. Then, when she realized no one else was smiling, she added, "Well, it's true."

The girl beside Sivya went next. She had on an outrageously colorful outfit, her long brown hair wound around her head with multicolored ribbons. She wore a dress over two more skirts, and her fingernails were each painted a different color. It made Georgia feel epileptic.

"And g'day, I'm Mikki Abbott. You can probably guess I'm Aussie, from Melbourne to be exact, and I'm stoked to be here. The Photography internship is choice. Did I say I was stoked? I take pictures, and also I paint. And I sculpt. Also, I do collages. I think I put one in my application portfolio . . ."

Her mentor, Lynn, gave a nod. "It was stunning, in fact," she said.

"And I can belly dance as well, if anyone wants to see later . . ." Mikki's voice trailed off. "Go, or I'll keep talking," she said to the girl in the chair next to her, also a colorful one, with black hair in a razor-sharp bob, and blue tips.

"Nova Burke," she said quickly. "Fashion. I can't say I'm from too far away like these other girls—I live about thirty blocks uptown."

Her supervisor, Demetria, cut in before she could finish. "Please, Nova, tell us a little more about your background in fashion." Her voice was like ice—it was clear from the get-go that she would be a hard one to impress. "For a start, who are your favorite designers?"

Nova took a moment. It was clearly a test. Then she began rattling off names: "Right now I'm loving Stella McCartney, Zac Posen, Kenzie, Mizrahi, Florentina . . . Depends on the night, but sometimes I go for BCBG and even Heatherette. But if you want to know the truth"— she leaned forward toward Demetria, as if they were the only two in the room—"I like to find the unknowns at the consignment shops and flea markets downtown. Belle and Harper, X-Ray Vision, Caliente, Zuzie, I could go on. This top is a classic, vintage Chanel, but I deconstructed it, changed the neck, added texture . . ."

"And what made you think you could do that?" Demetria asked. Her eyes were locked with her intern's.

Ms. Bishop, far away at the head of the table, actually seemed amused. She smiled at Nova, awaiting her explanation.

"Fashion is personal," Nova said. "The most cutting-edge people never wear straight off the rack. They always take a piece and make it their own." She stood up.

Georgia realized she was holding her breath. *Is she going to fight her boss here, on her very first day?!*

But no. Nova just turned around to show Demetria the back of her shirt. "See?" she said. "I sew. I've been altering my clothes since I was a kid. I've been learning some new appliqué techniques recently, which is how I did this."

Demetria nodded once. "I appreciate the shirt."

"I do as well," said Ms. Bishop, a faint smile still on her lips. "Now, who do we have next? Of course, Georgia."

No introductions were necessary, Georgia assumed, but she plunged in anyway. Yes, she was Molly Mack. Yes, she had a house in the Hollywood Hills, which is where the famous Hollywood sign on all the postcards is. Yes, even though she was a successful actress, she wanted to start a new career in magazine journalism.

Should I have said how much I want to be a writer? she wondered. *Should I have told them how much I love the magazine?*

But it was too late, because it was Elizabeth's turn, and she was off and running.

"I'm Elizabeth Cheekwood," she said. "I—I don't know where to begin." She turned to Ms. Bishop for help.

Georgia almost scoffed—until Ms. Bishop took up the plea and answered!

"Elizabeth was featured in *Publishers Weekly*," Ms. Bishop announced. "She's had some great luck with her first novel. Go on," she said to Elizabeth. "Tell them."

"Oh, yes," said Elizabeth, "I'm so very lucky."

Please, not this again.

Elizabeth continued, smiling sweetly at her fellow interns. "It's true that I sold my novel and I'll be working on it this summer. But also I'm here to intern with the Features department. To write. It's a dream come true to be here." She batted her long lashes at Ms. Bishop. Georgia thought she might gag.

Until she saw Ms. Bishop's brilliant smile. She was buying it! She thought the girl was as perfect as she pretended to be!

Now the drama of Georgia's summer was really taking shape. Everyone seemed nice and interesting, a good solid mix of a cast. Georgia—obviously—was the star, but a star always needs a nemesis. Someone who no one would think of at first as the bad guy (or girl). Clearly, Elizabeth was it.

ⓖ   ⓖ   ⓖ   ⓖ

You want in, newbie? Enter the password.

Georgia was back at her desk, and her computer was still possessed. The animated, pigtailed girl had returned with a vengeance. Now her big head was bouncing through a field of polka-dots. Georgia tried the password.

Error. Enter the password.

"I am!" Georgia shot out. Again she typed in the temporary password that was tacked up near her computer: "flirt." It wasn't working.

Georgia thought of Sivya. The girl was a self-proclaimed techno-geek; surely she could figure this out. And her cube was just on the other side of Georgia's.

Georgia peeked around the cubicle wall. "Sivya? How busy are you right now?"

Sivya rolled her chair closer. "Trey and I are going out to lunch, then we have a big meeting, but for now I'm free. Why?"

Georgia pointed to her computer. The pigtailed head was still bouncing.

"That's not the standard login," Sivya said, her interest immediately piqued. She took a seat in Georgia's chair and hit a few keys. The pigtailed head gave an extra-ferocious bounce. Sivya hit ESCAPE. Nothing. She tried some more keys, but nothing again. "This is not good," Sivya said at last. "Maybe we should call the IT department?"

Then they heard a low chuckle from the corridor. A guy walking past had stopped to get a closer look at Georgia's computer. "That's classic," he said, amused.

Georgia didn't like getting laughed at—not unless she was doing a comedy bit and having people laugh at you was the whole point. "Is this some kind of sick joke?" she said. "Haze the famous intern? So not funny." She gave the guy her don't-mess-with-me eyes. They were killer on camera. She just hoped they translated in real life.

Maybe so, because the guy stopped chuckling and held out his hand for a shake. "I'm Shawn, assistant editor in the Photography department. And you're obviously Georgia Cooper. I swear I had nothing to do with that. But I think I know who did."

Georgia shook Shawn's hand. So did Sivya. Shawn was grinning, still trying not to laugh. Georgia couldn't help but take note of how cute he was, even though she was annoyed at him for finding the situation so funny. He was in his twenties and—with the faux-hawk and the deep blue eyes—somewhat striking. Georgia was so over the played out faux-hawk . . . but she did admit it still looked good on certain guys. Shawn was one.

The pigtailed head on screen bopped around like a manic puppy. "Who did it, then?" Georgia asked. "Not the Entertainment editor who got axed?"

If so, no wonder Ms. Bishop fired her. She was a total freak!

"Not quite," Shawn said. He entered her cubicle. "First, gossip. You're dying to know what happened to the Entertainment editor, aren't you?"

"Yeah!" said Sivya in a whisper. "Tell us!"

"Her name's Belle Holder," Shawn began. "She used to write for *Rolling Stone*."

Sivya looked blank, like she'd never even heard the name, but Georgia nodded impatiently. Of course she knew who Belle Holder was—Georgia was a magazine junkie, duh.

Shawn gathered them in so their heads were close. He spoke in a low voice, playing it up like a ghost story around a campfire: It turned out that Belle Holder, star of her game, had betrayed *Flirt* by selling her intern's work to the competition. Her *intern's* work, not even hers. Ms. Bishop turned vicious, and Belle turned vicious right back, and it ended up with Belle having to gather her things and be escorted out of the building. Of course, as far as the media knew, all that happened between them were the usual "creative differences."

"And ever since then," Shawn continued, "they can't find anyone to take her spot. Ms. Bishop hired some guy, and he quit after a few weeks. He said he was selling all his stuff and moving to Thailand. Some other woman took the job and then changed her mind, so no one got to meet her. Ms. Bishop keeps interviewing people, but word is she's never satisfied."

Sivya stood up to look over Georgia's cubicle wall toward the Entertainment editor's empty office. The door was closed, the name tag beside it blank.

"What does this have to do with my computer problem?" Georgia said. "So there's been no Entertainment editor. So what?"

"Because guess who thought she ran the department until just a few weeks ago?" Shawn said. "The intern before you. Kiyoko. Her." He pointed at the bouncing head.

Sivya giggled, but Georgia was far from amused.

Shawn explained, "Last summer's interns ended up staying the whole year—they were that good. As for Kiyoko . . . after Belle left, she thought she was running the show. When she finally left, she said there'd be no Entertainment intern half as good as she was. Sorry, Georgia, but it looks like you've got a lot to live up to."

"That's not fair!" Sivya burst out. "Georgia just got here."

"I'm not about to run a whole department," Georgia said. "My ego's not *that* big."

"Hey, I didn't say I agreed with Kiyoko," Shawn said, winking at Georgia. "Who could compete with the infamous Molly Mack, anyway?"

"Thanks," Georgia said. "But this internship isn't a competition."

That's what she said out loud, but that sure wasn't what she was thinking.

I'll show this other intern, whoever she is, she thought, all fired up. Now she had not just Elizabeth to contend with, but also the legend of Kiyoko.

"What did you say the other intern's name was?" Sivya said suddenly.

"Kiyoko. She's Japanese."

"How do you spell that?"

"K-I-Y-O-K-O."

Sivya typed it into Georgia's computer and an animated scroll of text showed up: **That's right, beyotch! Say my name.**

"There," Sivya told Georgia. "You're all logged in."

Shawn shook his head. "She's unreal," he said. "Hope you interns this summer are just as fun." Then he gave a final wave and walked away.

"Thanks," Georgia said. Finally she could use her computer.

"It was nothing," Sivya said. "I hope they find a new Entertainment editor soon."

Georgia batted her lashes, keeping her face blank. "I'll be fine," she said.

"Okay," Sivya said. "I'm going to get ready for lunch with Trey. I bet I'll need to take notes. See you later?"

Georgia nodded. When Sivya was at last gone, she gathered her bearings. There was an e-mail in her inbox from Ms. Bishop.

Research Entertainment subjects. Specifically movie-related. We'll meet tomorrow to discuss. —JB

Research how? And, um, where?

Georgia needed more direction. Where was her director with the megaphone telling her where to stand and what marks to hit? Sivya had Trey. Asha had Naomi. Nailah had Gayle. Mikki had Lynn. Nova had Demetria (not that anyone would want Demetria).

Elizabeth had Ms. Bishop. Until someone new was hired, Georgia was supposed to have Ms. Bishop, too!

Georgia maneuvered through the maze of cubicles and somehow found her way to the editor-in-chief's office, which was along the wall of wide windows. She entered the antechamber but was stopped at once by Delia, who physically leaped out from behind her desk to keep Georgia from going in.

"I need to see Ms. Bishop," Georgia said. "It's important."

Then the phones starting ringing on Delia's desk—two lines at once—and she slipped back there, her hand still out. "Just wait there a moment," she told Georgia. "Ms. Bishop's in a meeting." She grabbed a ringing phone.

Georgia took a seat in the chair closest to Ms. Bishop's door. The door was open just a crack, and she could hear someone talking inside.

" Where was her director with the megaphone telling her where to stand and what marks to hit? "

"I do have high hopes for the summer. We have a lot of talent here . . ."

That was Ms. Bishop—she had to be talking about the interns.

"But . . ." someone else—a man—started. Georgia thought she recognized Quinn Carson's voice, the managing editor. "But what's your concern?" he said.

"These new girls have a lot to live up to. All six of our former interns will have pieces featured in the next issue—it's quite impressive."

"They were a standout group. Not to say that this group isn't—"

"Of course they are. I chose them for a reason. However, our previous interns truly raised the bar. We can't expect a repeat of last year. It simply wouldn't be fair."

"True."

"Although, I must admit, I am excited to see what Elizabeth Cheekwood will bring to the table. That's why I went out of my way to recruit her. She is quite a talent."

Elizabeth. Again.

Ms. Bishop had recruited her for the internship? What did that mean—did Elizabeth even have to apply?

Georgia had had enough. She left her chair and approached Delia's desk. "When is Ms. Bishop's meeting over?" she asked.

Delia paused mid-phone call. "Be patient, Georgia.

She'll finish with Quinn soon. Then she might have five minutes for you."

"Never mind. I'll come back later."

"You said it was important." Delia looked annoyed.

"Just . . . never mind." Georgia headed back to her cube. She had a whole lot of "research" to do. And, if the conversation she'd overheard between Ms. Bishop and Quinn was any indication, it wouldn't matter how hard she worked on her project or any project this summer. No one could live up to last year's superstar interns, except maybe Elizabeth. Georgia didn't have the starring role. She was the mid-season replacement.

"Aarrgh!" Georgia said aloud when she reached her desk. Her screensaver was a litter of bouncing Kiyokos. First things first: Get a new screensaver. Then do some brilliant research and prove Ms. Bishop wrong. How hard could that be?

chapter two

The girls, and all their luggage, were driven to their new summer home in two separate limousines. Elizabeth felt like the luckiest girl in the world. Incredible things kept happening to her. First, her articles started getting published in magazines. Then her dad had a friend who had a friend who was a literary agent, and that agent, Constance Gack, signed Elizabeth even though she'd written only three chapters of her novel. Then Josephine Bishop of *Flirt* magazine called to ask if Elizabeth might be interested in her internship program—Elizabeth barely had to apply. And now she was gliding in a limo through the streets of Manhattan like a VIP. It was fantastic.

Elizabeth was determined to make this a summer to remember. She'd write for *Flirt*, and that would look great on her Princeton application. In her off-hours she'd explore the city and have some fun for once. Like tonight, her first night in New York . . . she wanted to go out! She wanted to experience! She wanted to find a cool club and go dancing!

She never did anything like that back home in Virginia. It wasn't because her parents were too strict—they had no reason to be. Elizabeth was a good girl, always had been. She was a straight-A student. She had a nice group of friends all headed for the Ivies. None of her friends broke curfew or lied to their parents to go out partying. There was dancing, but only at slumber parties, and parents were always monitoring the noise level downstairs. Elizabeth was sixteen and she went to bed—voluntarily!—by ten o'clock.

At school, Elizabeth overheard other girls talking, girls she wasn't friends with. They'd stand around the bathrooms, between or during classes, in no rush to get where they were going. They talked about clubs they'd been to in D.C., how they'd snagged their fake IDs, what they'd said to convince their parents they were studying American history at the library instead of crashing a frat party.

How exciting it sounded.

Just before the school year ended, Elizabeth had bumped into some of the cool girls during fourth-period trigonometry. This was in the upstairs bathroom, where the seniors hung out. Elizabeth came in with her bathroom pass and found a few of them skipping class. They were talking about taking a trip to New York that summer. Elizabeth couldn't help herself. "I'm going to New York this summer, too," she burst out.

The coolest of the seniors, a girl named Jasmine, raised an eyebrow. "With your mother?" she said. Most of the kids at school knew that Elizabeth's mother worked in politics.

"Oh, no—by myself," Elizabeth said. She told them

about the internship, getting a little flutter in her stomach when she noticed how impressed they were. "And I'll check out all the cool clubs while I'm there," she bragged. "Every one."

Jasmine seemed surprised. "You go clubbing?"

"Oh, yeah," Elizabeth said. "I mean, I'm going to."

"You'll have to tell us *all* about it," Jasmine said, like she wouldn't believe it until she heard details. The seniors flounced out of the bathroom, and Elizabeth hurried to get back to trig before she missed the review equations.

Even now, she kept recalling that brief conversation. No one thought she was capable of doing anything remotely crazy. Not her parents. Not her friends. Not anyone except Elizabeth herself—maybe, sometimes.

It wasn't that she wanted to impress those other girls, not really. What she wanted was something to talk about. She wanted to have had a *life*—not just write about people who did.

She turned to the other two girls sharing her limo. "So," she said, "what do you guys want to do tonight?"

"Sleep," Asha said. "Today was intense. I could sleep for an entire week."

"I'm knackered as well," Nailah said quietly. "I must have jet lag."

Count them out for dancing, Elizabeth thought. She'd had high hopes for Georgia. That girl had to know all the good clubs—she'd been photographed at a few of them. However, Georgia hadn't been enthusiastic that morning when Elizabeth had brought up the idea. In fact, she'd been sort of mean. Elizabeth decided to set her sights on Nova. She was from Manhattan; she would know what was going on that night.

Elizabeth had wanted to be in the same limo as Nova so she could ask, but she'd ended up in the limo with Nailah and Asha, and they weren't even from this country.

The driver—his name was Jared—stopped the limo at a cobblestone curb before a large cast-iron building that seemed to be made almost entirely of windows. "Welcome to SoHo," he said, "and to your loft."

The girls thanked Jared and, in minutes, had lugged their bags into the elevator and were ooohing and ahhhing over the top-floor loft where they'd be living all summer. Their housemother, Emma Lyric, was there to welcome them. She said that she had a son who usually lived in the loft, too, but he was on a study-abroad trip to Rome for the summer. She explained that she had some rules they'd need to follow, most specifically curfew, but she could hardly get a word in edgewise amid all the excitement.

All the windows made the enormous main room of the loft, still bright as day in the early July evening, light up from the setting sun. The main room had enough space to put in a roller rink. It was furnished with couches, chairs, window seats, a full dining table and chairs, a chef's kitchen, even a few nooks for quiet reading. Elizabeth was in awe.

Only one person wasn't in awe: Georgia. "Is this it?" she asked. She stood beside a mountain of matching luggage—her things had been delivered to the loft that morning.

Emma burst out laughing. She seemed at ease with the girls, like an older sister there just to make sure they didn't burn the place down. She had amber shoulder-length hair and freckles, and was dressed like a teenager in Lucky jeans and a soft cotton tee. "Yes, this is it, our tiny little loft!" she told Georgia. "Plus, you girls will be sharing the bedrooms upstairs." She indicated the spiral staircase that led to the second floor.

"I'm serious," Georgia said. "What if I need some privacy to write, or think?"

Emma narrowed her eyes. "Then you can go out on the fire escape. Or on the roof."

"I was just asking," Georgia snapped.

Elizabeth thought the whole Molly Mack thing was cooler than cool—imagine, living all summer with a TV star!—but still, Georgia didn't have to act like the world revolved around her.

Emma continued. "Besides, I thought Elizabeth here was the

66 This is it, our tiny little loft! 99

writer, and she doesn't seem upset about privacy. That's you, isn't it?" Emma asked, a welcoming smile on her face.

"I can write anywhere," Elizabeth assured Emma. "Don't worry about me." She smiled at Georgia, but Georgia was so far from smiling, she was scowling.

What did I do? Elizabeth thought.

Elizabeth went to find Nova. "Hi," she said, coming upon her on one of the window seats at the far end of the giant room. Nova was turned away, checking the text messages on her cell phone.

"Hey," Nova said without looking up. She laughed to herself as if one of her texts was really funny and started punching in a message back.

"Can I talk to you?" Elizabeth persisted.

Nova put her phone down. "What's up?" Her blue and black hair, plus her dark eye makeup, made her a little intimidating, but Elizabeth forged on.

"I was wondering . . ." Now Elizabeth was starting to feel shy. "What's going on tonight? I mean, what are our plans?"

"*Our* plans? I didn't know we had plans," Nova said.

"I was thinking maybe we could go to a club."

"Sorry. I'm meeting some friends. You go, have fun." She returned to her phone to finish her text message. When Elizabeth didn't move, she looked up, seeming impatient. "What? Did you want something else?"

"No," Elizabeth said automatically.

Will I have to go out by myself? Nah. More likely, I'll spend the night in, doing nothing special, like always.

Elizabeth swallowed her disappointment. She was used to this. Truly, it was silly of her to think she was the kind of girl to go off running into the night in a strange city just to have some so-called fun. Elizabeth Cheekwood wouldn't do that. Elizabeth Cheekwood, the one who got this internship, not to mention the book deal, would probably go to bed early.

Now Emma was calling all the girls over to show them the housewarming presents that had been left behind by the previous interns. There were neighborhood maps with the best cafés circled, cinema coupons, and even an unlimited MetroCard someone had no longer needed.

Also, there were notes. Former Beauty intern Genevieve Bishop had left Asha a lemon yellow notecard that read: *To the new Beauty intern, Have a fun summer. Naomi Wu is a decent boss. Just a few words of advice: My Aunt Jo has high standards, so be warned. And steer clear of any celebrity hair assignments. You'll thank me later. —Gen*

"I wonder what that means," Asha said. "The hair assignments must be complex."

"Her aunt, huh?" Nova said in a low voice. "Wonder how *she* got the internship."

"Oh, stop," Emma said. "There's no hint of nepotism

this summer. And as for the 'celebrity hair assignment,' Gen's still sore about a little mishap with Alice Ayers—"

"That was an *intern*?" Georgia burst in. "I heard about that. She didn't get fired?"

"No, she did not get fired," Emma said. "Now, Mikki, this one's for you."

Mikki's letter from the former Photography intern Alexa Veron was really a photo collage using pictures of found letters from the street. Different signs spelled out, letter by letter, *WELCOME TO NYC, FLIRTISTA!*

"Cute," Mikki said. "Where do I know that name, Alexa Veron?"

"She's a model," Nova said. "For Bjorn V."

"True," Emma said. "But before she was a model— and during, actually—she was an intern at *Flirt*. See what crazy things might turn up for you girls this summer? Nova, this one's yours."

Nova inspected a letter with the words *Fashion Intern* on the top. She skimmed the page quickly. "I'll read it later," she said.

"Is the Fashion intern a famous model, too?" Sivya asked. "Or, let me guess, a movie star." She winked at Georgia.

"Nope," Nova said. "Sounds like she's an apprentice at Florentina. I'm impressed." She didn't look impressed. Nova had such a blasé manner about everything, Elizabeth wondered if she ever showed any emotion.

The next note was from Charlotte Gabel, the former intern for two separate departments—Health and Fitness, and Electronic Content. She had sensible advice for both Nailah and Sivya, such as how Trey liked his messages organized and during what hours Gayle would be most open for brainstorming.

Elizabeth's note was from former Features intern Melanie Henderson, a looooong letter, so long it needed an oversize envelope.

"Did she write a novel for the novelist?" Mikki teased.

"Don't worry, I'll read it later and paraphrase for you guys," Elizabeth said. "So we just have one more to go . . . Georgia's."

Everyone looked at the empty table. "That's, uh, the thing," Emma said. "The previous interns set up this whole plan to leave little notes of advice for you—although in Mel's case it certainly wasn't little!—but Kiyoko, the Entertainment intern, she can be a bit forgetful at times."

Georgia shrugged. "Whatever. I don't need a note."

"I don't think Kiyoko forgot," Sivya said. She gave Georgia a sidelong glance, then continued. "Kiyoko locked up Georgia's computer with . . . I guess you could call it a note. Thankfully, we figured out the password."

"It was so immature," Georgia announced. "I doubt I'd want her advice, anyway. She seems like a freak."

Emma didn't argue. "So, let's go see your rooms, and then—since I know *I'm* starving—I ordered pizza! It's already on the way."

Most of the girls cheered at the thought of their first New York–style pizza, except two. Nova seemed her usual unexcited self. "Pizza's good," she said, shrugging. "Maybe later I'll order in some Thai." And Nailah, who, it turned out, did not eat cheese, or anything that was not 100 percent whole grain, spoke up to ask questions about what specific ingredients were on the pizzas and what oils they used to cook with.

"I also ordered a salad," Emma said, trying to appease her. "And Nova, I'm sure the other interns left a Thai menu around here somewhere."

Nova shrugged again. "Pizza's fine."

Nailah said gratefully, "Salad is exactly what I wanted. Thank you, Emma."

The girls sped up the spiral stairs to take a look at the bedrooms. "Wait, wait!" Emma called after them. "We need to pick roommates!"

She reached the landing and indicated the three doors. "Three rooms, seven girls. Usually the internship program accepts six girls, but as you can see, this summer . . . we have one extra. So one room will have to triple up. I have all your names on slips of paper here. I just need . . ."

"A hat!" Sivya said. She grabbed one of her own caps and handed it to Emma.

"Here we go," Emma said, removing the names one at a time. "Room one—Nova and Asha. Room two—Elizabeth and Nailah. So that leaves, for room three, the biggest room here—Sivya, Mikki, and Georgia!"

Elizabeth smiled at her roommate, Nailah. She seemed nice enough. Although she also seemed really, really shy, and hadn't she mentioned in the limo that she was tired and wanted to go to sleep?

As the girls carried their suitcases up the stairs, someone was pitching a fit. Surprise—it was none other than Georgia Cooper. "Nova," she was saying, "don't you live uptown? Why do you even need a room? You don't, do you? You can go home whenever you want. Maybe you could take my spot in the three-person room and let me room with Asha?" She smiled brightly, as if her idea was pure genius.

But Nova wouldn't budge. "Just because my parents live uptown doesn't mean I have to stay with them. I'm living here." She dropped her suitcase on her bed.

"It was just an idea . . ." Georgia said. But she still wouldn't set foot in the three-person room, even though—Emma hadn't lied—it was a huge corner room with more than enough space to fit three girls. "You don't understand," she said to anyone who would listen. "I'm an only child. I have my own room, actually my own *house*. I mean, my mom lives there with me, but it was my Molly Mack money that bought it. I just don't know if I can do this, for real. I mean, seriously—there are more interns this summer, so *Flirt* should have built another room. You know what, maybe I'll stay in a hotel. I'm calling my manager."

Emma was concerned. "Georgia," she started, "please don't get upset—"

Elizabeth interrupted. "I'll trade with Georgia. She can have my room. I'll bunk with Mikki and Sivya."

"You don't mind?" Georgia said, brightening considerably.

"Elizabeth, really, you don't have to do that," Emma said.

"I don't mind," she said.

What she wanted was for everyone to like her, especially Georgia. Maybe it would soften things between them.

Georgia didn't say thanks. She just nodded as if she'd expected the sacrifice all along and went into her new room to claim her bed.

ⓖ   ⓖ   ⓖ   ⓖ

Over the dregs of pizza and salad, Mikki got the girls all pumped up. "This is going to be an incredible summer, you check? We'll be the best interns the magazine's ever seen."

"Yeah!" Sivya said.

Asha beamed. "I hope we do well," she said.

"To the best!" Mikki said, toasting with her bottle of grape soda.

"The best!" the girls chorused. Emma had left them alone, saying she'd be upstairs if they needed her, so after they all shrieked out the toast, they tried to quiet down.

Georgia cleared her throat. "Actually," she said, "I highly doubt that."

"And what's that supposed to mean?" Nova asked.

"I overheard Ms. Bishop talking to that managing editor guy, Quinn."

"So . . . ?" Asha prompted.

"So they're not too excited about us this summer. They said the interns from last year were, like, worlds better than we could ever be."

"Not funny," Mikki said.

"I didn't think so, either," Georgia said. She nibbled at her pizza crust, and then sighed.

She's serious, Elizabeth thought. The smile fell from her face.

"They really said that?" Sivya asked quietly. She looked crestfallen.

Georgia nodded with authority. "I heard the whole conversation. Did you know those interns from last summer were so great they ended up staying all year?"

"Howzat?" Mikki said. "I didn't even know that could happen."

"Tell me about it." Georgia looked straight at Elizabeth. "Lizzy," she said, "I'm so sorry to have to tell you this, but Ms. Bishop said that Melanie girl was the best writer she'd ever worked with. She called Melanie 'a talent.' I remember those exact words. She said it would be hard for you to live up. That really sucks. Sorry."

"Yeah," Elizabeth said, but she was having a hard time believing it. Of course Melanie Henderson was a talented writer—she wouldn't have thought otherwise. Yet Ms. Bishop had recruited Elizabeth for the internship herself. She wouldn't have called to ask Elizabeth to apply if she didn't think she'd be good.

Why would Georgia lie about something like that?

"That sucks," Nova said in a flat voice. She didn't seem upset, just resigned to the fact that she'd have to work harder.

All at once, Mikki bounded out of her chair and stood on top of the couch. "You know what? I say we prove them wrong! I say we rock the magazine, get them begging to keep us by September. What do you say, mates?"

"Okay," Asha and Sivya said. Nailah nodded. Nova shrugged.

"Lizzy?" Mikki said.

"Definitely," Elizabeth said, trying to be enthusiastic. Mikki kept bouncing up and down on the couch, filled with determined energy. It was catching. "Definitely!" she said again, this time much louder. She joined Mikki on the couch.

Georgia took the last few nibbles of her pizza crust, looking amused.

 ❍   ❍   ❍   ❍

To the LUCKY new Features intern:
Hi! I'm Melanie Henderson (call me Mel). I'm one of the interns Ms. Bishop worked to the bone for a whole year, and man, was it worth it! No joke. So listen, I have tons of advice. If I don't answer all your questions in this letter (and I've got a feeling this'll be a long letter), just e-mail me at melwrites247@freemail.com. I'm traveling to Rome to visit my boyfriend, but I am so totally available by e-mail! So, first things first, your new boss, Ms. Bishop. She's tough, I won't lie. She'll make you write 12 drafts of an article before she's satisfied, she'll assign you impossible deadlines that you'll have to (you'll HAVE to) meet, she'll critique your commas till you want to cry, and don't be freaked by her heavy use of the red pen (she loooooooves that red pen). But guess what? It's all worth it. If you want to impress Bishop, all you have to do is —

"You're still reading that thing?" a voice cut in. Elizabeth found Mikki standing over her, wearing an emerald green halter dress with purple lace-up sandals. "Nova's agreed to let us go out with her," Mikki said, her eyes all sparkly. "The other girls say they're too zonked to go. What say you?"

"Are you kidding? Of course I want to go," Elizabeth said. She dropped the letter and bounded off her bed.

Yes!

Nova was downstairs, lacing up her boots. Georgia was lounging on one of the couches, an eye mask shielding her eyes from the lamplight. Asha and Sivya were sharing another couch, reading.

"You in?" Nova said to Elizabeth, like she didn't care one way or the other.

"Are we going clubbing?" Elizabeth said. "I read about this one place online—I think it was called Pink Bunny, or Pink Pumpkin? Pink something. Is that where we're going?"

"You mean the Pink Pony? That's a coffeehouse, not a club," Nova said. "You can go wherever you want. I told you I already had plans. My friends and I are going to this all-ages show on Bowery. My friend's band is playing. Nothing too exciting." She shrugged. "You guys can tag along if you want."

Mikki looked excited enough to jump back on the couch. "We are so there. You know what? We should all go. What do you say, mates?"

"Hmmmm," Asha said. She held up a chemistry

textbook. "Did I tell you that my parents have me taking an advanced chemistry course at NYU this summer? I have two chapters to read before the session starts . . ."

"You'd rather read about grimy old chemistry than go hear Nova's friend's band play?" Mikki said. "That's not polite, Asha."

Asha looked stricken. "I didn't mean to be rude . . ."

"The band isn't that good," Nova said offhandedly. She finished lacing up her boots.

"I'll go," Sivya burst out.

Nailah's bare feet could be seen from behind a couch. She was doing some sort of yoga move that involved balancing precariously upside down. At least Elizabeth assumed it was yoga. "Nailah, are you in? Nailah?" she called.

Nailah spoke from her spot upside down. "Emma said curfew is eleven."

"Bowery is, like, really close. I'm walking it," Nova said. "And I'm leaving in fifteen. So hurry up if you want

> ❝ Nailah's bare feet could be seen from behind a couch. She was doing some sort of yoga move that involved balancing precariously upside down. At least Elizabeth assumed it was yoga. ❞

to go." She headed upstairs, and Mikki and Sivya followed. After a beat, Nailah righted herself and went, too.

"I shouldn't . . ." Asha said. "You're not going, are you, Lizzy? Didn't you say you have some pages of your novel to write?"

"Yeah, that's true . . ." Elizabeth said. She *had* told the girls she had to work on her novel, because she did. Really. But one night wouldn't ruin anything.

"So you're going, then?" Asha asked.

Of course Elizabeth was going. This would be her first shot at hearing a live band play. She'd been to a concert once—Billy Joel, with her parents, so she didn't think it counted.

"Oh, Lizzy's going for sure. That's why she's here this summer, to have fun," Georgia said. She removed her eye mask. "Maybe I'll tag along, too."

Elizabeth couldn't tell if she was being nice or fake nice or just plain mean. Then she decided she didn't care. Her first night in New York and she was already doing something new. "I can't wait," she said. "I'm dying to go out dancing!"

Nova was coming back down the stairs—her eyelids slathered in a haze of gray, like shimmering smog. "I didn't say anything about dancing . . ." she said.

◎   ◎   ◎   ◎

Nova was right about the dancing—it was more like slamming. A crowd with spiky hair and sharp objects attached to their clothes smacked against one another, crushing up against the stage. Elizabeth could barely see past them, let alone dance. Mikki and Sivya and Elizabeth did try to make a go of it, but after five minutes of jostling—and, in the case of Sivya, an elbow to the ribs—they headed for their table in the back of the dark club. All the interns had decided to go, even Asha, and they sat around the tiny table, straining to hear one another over the noise of the band.

"Is this the kind of place Nova goes to often?" Elizabeth yelled to the girls. Nova was all the way across the club, hanging with her friends at the side of the stage. She wasn't being very inclusive.

"I think she goes anywhere there's a party," Mikki yelled.

"My fans'll be so shocked when they see me here," Georgia yelled. "Everyone knows punk is dead." Then she stood and craned her neck to gaze around the club. "But at least those paparazzi didn't follow us in, huh?"

A few photographers had caught pictures of "Molly Mack" while they were standing in line outside the club. Even though Georgia had made a big show of acting annoyed when she first saw them, she'd posed for numerous pictures without complaint.

Asha looked so out of place in the dark corner of

the club that it couldn't have been worse had she brought her chem book.

That was me, Elizabeth thought. *But this summer there's going to be a new me.*

Mikki grabbed her sleeve. "I'm going to the bar. Come with."

Elizabeth didn't have to be asked twice.

They snaked through the crowd, avoiding elbows. Like a pro, Mikki shoved her way up to the bar. "What've you got on tap, mate?" she yelled to the bartender. He named some beers Elizabeth had never heard of—not that she'd heard of many, seeing as she'd never had a drink before. Like ever.

"You're drinking beer?" Elizabeth yelled to Mikki, surprised.

"Yeah," Mikki answered. "Hey, what do you want?"

"I don't think I'd *like* beer." She'd heard it tasted pretty nasty.

"No worries—maybe you'll like an apple cider, then." Mikki ordered the two drinks, and maybe it was her cute Aussie accent and the way she called him "mate"—which is what she called everybody she met—but the bartender blatantly ignored the underage stamp on her hand and served her the two bottles.

Back at the table, Elizabeth sipped at her cider. It wasn't until she found herself grinning maniacally, the music making her legs and arms perform a little dance in her seat, that she realized there was something off about her apple cider. She checked the bottle. It was hard cider with—the label said—even more alcoholic content than beer! No wonder she was all giggly and chilled out.

She didn't pay much attention to Nova's friend's band. In fact, she wasn't sure which of the bands had Nova's friend in it. She had another cider. She ignored Asha's wide-eyed look as she drank it, and Georgia's smirk. Mikki was a lot of fun. They talked (yelled, really) about art and writing and life, and when all the girls were running back to the loft to make the eleven o'clock curfew, Elizabeth even made Mikki stop on a corner to give her a crash course in belly dancing.

Life moves fast in New York City. It was Elizabeth's first night there, and already she'd had her first drink of alcohol, danced at a punk show, almost missed curfew, and had a blast the whole time. No one from home would recognize her. This new Elizabeth was tons of fun. Who would have guessed?

꘧   ꘧   ꘧   ꘧

The new Elizabeth also had a headache the next morning. The girls had been called to Ms. Bishop's office to learn about their first project. They were waiting in the antechamber, notebooks and pens at the ready. Elizabeth felt a little woozy.

She leaned over to Mikki. "Do I have a hangover?" she asked innocently.

Mikki cracked up. "From two ciders? Doubt that."

"Heh," Georgia said, overhearing. Elizabeth's possible hangover seemed to cheer her considerably. She'd been acting moody since a paparazzi photographer had followed her into the subway and she'd found a post about it on Stalkerazzi.com titled "Molly Mack slums it on the N train" when they reached the office just thirty minutes later.

"Elizabeth, you should take things more seriously," Georgia said loudly. "If Ms. Bishop finds out about last night—oh, good morning, Ms. Bishop. How are you today?"

"Just fine, Georgia," Ms. Bishop said. She'd arrived without a sound, the plush white carpeting silencing her stilettos. "And how are all of you?" she asked the other interns, her gaze holding on Elizabeth a beat longer than the rest.

Can she tell? Elizabeth thought. But before she could mull the matter over any further, Ms. Bishop was ushering the girls into her office. And what an office it was. The main color scheme was white, just like the antechamber—sleek white furniture, white couches and chairs, white desk, white computer, white high-reaching walls.

The girls took seats at a long table overlooking Times Square and sat quietly. Elizabeth could tell that they were feeling weird around Ms. Bishop, after what Georgia had told them. Ms. Bishop didn't seem to notice anything, though—maybe she was used people waiting for her to speak.

"You are about to work on a project very close to my heart," Ms. Bishop announced, handing a stack of photocopies to each intern. "Consider yourselves lucky. Now, what each of you has is what we call the current book, the 'New Faces in Fashion' issue of the magazine, my favorite theme in all the years we've published *Flirt*, in fact. This one will feature a portfolio of new designers' work as well as pieces on up-and-coming actors and musicians and artists. This issue must be wrapped up in two weeks. We're working down to the wire to fill it. Now"—she clapped her hands together, completely shocking Sivya, who bolted upright as if caught napping—"I have room for a few more pieces—no promises, but there is time for an intern to make her first splash in this issue. If she's lucky. So study the book and we'll meet to discuss your ideas."

"How long do we have?" Sivya asked.

"Hours," Ms. Bishop said. "I want to hear ideas as soon as possible. We'll meet in a few days to discuss pitches. Delia will e-mail you the details."

"I'm stoked," Mikki said quickly. "We all are."

"Thank you, Ms. Bishop," Asha added.

Seeming satisfied, Ms. Bishop nodded. "And keep your schedules free for the night of July fourth," she said.

"For what?" Mikki asked.

"*Flirt*'s annual Fourth of July party," Ms. Bishop said with a tight smile. "The interns always attend. It's just the first of many perks."

Nova, totally out of character, got a huge smile on her face. "The party on the East River?" she said.

"That's the one," Ms. Bishop said.

"Nice!" Nova said under her breath.

The girls gathered their papers and started for the door. Then Ms. Bishop called out, "Georgia, I expect you back here at eleven. Elizabeth, stay."

Elizabeth froze mid-step. When the other girls had left, Ms. Bishop asked her to shut the door behind them.

"What is the problem, then?" Ms. Bishop asked.

"Um, I don't think there's a problem," Elizabeth said.

"Georgia mentioned something. About last night?" Ms. Bishop prompted.

Elizabeth shrugged. "Georgia was just kidding. Nothing happened last night."

"All right—I trust you'll come to me directly if you have a problem." She held her gaze on Elizabeth, securing her deep in her seat. "I have high hopes for you this summer. I wouldn't have recruited you otherwise."

Elizabeth smiled graciously. She wasn't sure who to trust, Georgia or Ms. Bishop, but she wanted to trust Ms. Bishop.

"I am expecting an article from you to run in the 'New Faces' issue—so show me something worth publishing."

"I will, I promise," Elizabeth said.

"Now, for your assignments." Ms. Bishop produced a stack of items that needed doing, including packages to send to VIPs, photocopies to be made, and faxes to be sent. She went over each project thoroughly, barely giving Elizabeth a chance to get a word in.

Elizabeth had been excited about the vote of confidence Ms. Bishop had shown her, but now she was getting concerned. *How much does she think I can handle in my first week?* she thought.

In the hallway, Elizabeth ran into Georgia, who was heading to Ms. Bishop's for her eleven o'clock meeting.

"How's the hangover?" Georgia said, too loudly.

"It's not a hangover. Mikki said that's not possible," Elizabeth whispered. "I just have a headache, and it's practically gone now. But Georgia, look at all this stuff Ms. Bishop wants me to do. Plus come up with an article for the 'New Faces' issue. I have to go to the mailroom now and stuff envelopes!"

"What did you expect, a free ride?" Georgia said. Then her face softened and she leaned in closer. "What's your article about, anyway?" She seemed pretty curious. Elizabeth wished she had something to tell her.

"Who knows," she said. "Maybe an idea will come

to me while I'm licking stamps. What are you writing? Is it about Hollywood?"

Georgia pulled back. "I'm not ready to talk about my idea yet. It's, you know, gesticulating."

"Do you mean *gestating*?" Elizabeth asked, trying to keep a straight face.

"You know what I mean," Georgia said darkly. "I've got to go. I shouldn't keep Ms. Bishop waiting."

Elizabeth tried not to laugh as Georgia hurried away.

    ⓖ   ⓖ   ⓖ   ⓖ

In the mailroom, Elizabeth ran into Asha. She was sorting makeup samples into piles. Once sorted, they would be packed up with a complimentary issue of *Flirt*.

"It's so glamorous being an intern," Asha joked as some packing tape got stuck to her fingers.

Elizabeth helped her pull it off only to get the tape caught on her own shirt. They giggled, covering their mouths to keep quiet. "I know," Elizabeth said. "Look at all these packages Ms. Bishop wants me to put together. After this, I'll be the best envelope-stuffer at Princeton University!"

Asha stopped sorting the mini lipsticks. "Are you applying to Princeton?"

"I sort of have to. I'm a legacy," Elizabeth said, shrugging. "Are you applying there, too?"

"It's on my list. You know—Harvard, Yale, Columbia,

Princeton. If I go to college here in the States, my parents want it to be at one of the top universities."

"Sounds like my parents," Elizabeth said. "Did they let you take this internship only because it would look good on your college application?"

"The opposite, actually," Asha said. "They really didn't want me to take the internship. I had to beg for weeks. It was only after they learned that the advanced chem course at NYU could count for pre-college credit that they agreed. According to them, that course is my priority this summer. The internship comes second."

"Then don't tell them about stuffing envelopes. That's not college prep."

"So true."

Elizabeth had a lot in common with Asha. They both had parents with through-the-roof expectations, and they both did all they could to live up to them. Asha was a good girl; that was obvious. So was Elizabeth—at least until last night, when she'd downed two whole ciders and slam danced in a crowd of punk rockers with cheek piercings! If that was Asha's first real impression of her, then she had no idea what Elizabeth was really like.

Maybe what Elizabeth needed to do this summer was work hard to impress Ms. Bishop. And also complete her novel, which was technically due to her agent before she returned to school in the fall.

She could have fun in college. Or after. She could

have fun when she was twenty-five.

Elizabeth let out a loud sigh. "Asha, don't you ever want to, oh, I don't know, drop the class and just have fun this summer?" she asked tentatively.

Asha laughed. "Chemistry can be fun! You just have to be creative about it. Take these lipsticks, for example. From what I learned in chemistry class, I could create lipstick, any color I wanted. Sometimes I do experiments like that. To me, that's fun."

"Then why don't you?" Elizabeth said.

"Why don't I what? Make lip balm?"

Elizabeth shrugged. "Shouldn't you get to do what *you* want for once, and not just what everyone else wants?"

Asha had an intense look on her face. "Lizzy, you make a good point," she said. "Perhaps I will."

⟲　　⟲　　⟲　　⟲

"Emma is one choice housemother," Mikki was saying. "D'you know she's a photographer? I love her already. And another reason I love her? She's letting me use her son's art studio since he's in Rome. You need to see the studio, mate. C'mon!"

Elizabeth had hardly gotten through the door to the interns' loft before Mikki was dragging her up the stairs and into the private apartment Emma kept on the second floor.

Sure enough, Mikki had taken over the art studio. There were Mikki's tubes of paint, her cutouts from newspapers and magazines, a bowl of something that looked like papier-mâché, and a scattering of photographs, some painted on and some gouged in strategic places with pins. Mikki's chosen color palette included shades of blue and green, with a few touches of bright yellow and orange. The room was a mess. But it was a mess brimming with creative energy. Just being around Mikki made Elizabeth want to be creative, too. It reminded her why she'd wanted to write a novel in the first place.

Mikki's long hair was wild down her back, and blue paint was speckled here and there in her curls. She had a piece of collage stuck to her cheek.

"So what do you think, mate?" Mikki said.

"I love it," Elizabeth said honestly.

"There's more." Mikki led Elizabeth up a ladder to the rooftop of the building. There was a spectacular glimpse of the city's buildings, the other rooftops spreading out in various colors all around them. They found seats on the brick wall near a small vegetable garden.

Elizabeth breathed it in. *Look at where I am!* she thought, dazed and thrilled in equal measure. "I should come up here to write," she said.

"Speaking of writing," Mikki said, "I am so curious about your novel, mate. You've got to tell me about it."

"It's due at the end of the summer—the first draft,

anyway. I need to work on it while I'm here, when I have extra time . . . but Ms. Bishop also wants me to write an article, and that's due, and . . . I'll just have to find a way to juggle all my deadlines!" Elizabeth was keeping upbeat about the whole thing, mainly because Mikki was such a positive person. What Elizabeth didn't mention to Mikki was the sense of panic she was starting to feel deep in her gut. So far, it had been easy to ignore, but it was there. Maybe Asha could handle two things at once, but sometimes Elizabeth wasn't sure she could.

"That bloody sucks!" Mikki said. "I despise deadlines. I won't do 'em."

Elizabeth laughed. "Artists have deadlines. Photographers have deadlines. You'll get used to them."

"Doubt it. I can't work under a deadline, ever. It kills my creative process, yeah? I create what I want to create when I want to. I don't know how you do it, Lizzy."

Elizabeth shrugged. Truth is, she wasn't exactly doing it. Not yet.

Note to self: Get to work tonight! Think up some ideas for the Flirt *article. And write another chapter of the novel!*

"But you didn't answer my question," Mikki continued. "Your novel. What's it about, then?"

"It's an adventure story. International intrigue. 'Girl meets world' kind of thing."

"Sounds choice."

"It would be . . . if I had more written."

"Don't be so hard on yourself. You have an agent and everything. So probably it's almost done, yeah?"

"Not exactly. Honest truth? I wrote three chapters, like, months ago. I haven't written anything new since."

"And it's due end of summer?" Mikki asked.

Elizabeth nodded.

"You can do it! What you need is just one creative spark. Then you'll write it in one weekend. That's how it is for me. I get inspired, work all night, and then I have my masterpiece." She winked. "Maybe not *master*piece."

"Yeah, I just need inspiration." Elizabeth willed herself to get up and do something. "And motivation."

Mikki shook her by the shoulders. "What're you doing, mate?! Go down to the flat and write. Or write up here, under the stars." She gazed upward at the smoggy city sky. "Not sure if we'll see stars tonight. But you get the picture."

"Maybe . . ." Elizabeth said. "Maybe if you hang out up here, too? Keep me company?"

Mikki's so creative, so alive. Just having her around will get me inspired.

"Nah," Mikki said. "Just got all pumped up to paint. I'm going down to the studio." She headed for the ladder.

Elizabeth hurried up to follow. "I'll join you. I'll set up my laptop in the corner of the studio. I'll write while you paint, it'll be—"

But Mikki stopped on the ladder. "Sos, Lizzy,

seriously sorry. But that won't work for me. I'm not one of those artists who needs a buddy. I can only do my art alone."

"Oh, okay," Elizabeth said. She hung back. "You know, I'll stay up here for a while. Maybe I'll get inspired, too."

Mikki waved and disappeared down the ladder.

Elizabeth returned to the brick wall and sat back down. Suddenly, without thinking, she burst out, "What am I doing?" The grating sound of her own voice shocked her.

It also shocked someone else—another someone who'd been up on the roof the whole time. "You just scared the snot out of me," Georgia said, appearing from behind the chimney with an iced tea in her hand.

"Sorry," Elizabeth said. "I—I don't know what came over me."

"So you've got only the three brilliant chapters of your novel and that's it, huh?" Georgia said. She was smiling a stiff little smile.

"Yes," Elizabeth admitted. "That's all I've got. Maybe my agent will just leave me alone this summer and let me focus on *Flirt* and I'll finish up the novel when I'm in school and . . ." She stopped talking. "I shouldn't be so stressed out."

"Not at all. I read about your book, you know. I Googled you. There's all this stuff about you online—you'd think you're the one who's famous or something."

"Yeah?" Elizabeth said.

"The idea is . . . good," Georgia said. She seemed reluctant to admit it. "I like adventure stories. So how'd you do the research?"

"Research?"

"For the book. Doesn't your character travel all over the world and do all these crazy things? You must have traveled a lot."

"Not really."

Georgia cocked her head, listening.

"That's sort of the problem. It's hard to write this whole action-packed story that takes place overseas when I haven't ever been anywhere or done anything, you know? I've never even been off the East Coast! Truth is, Georgia, I'm . . . I guess you could say I'm stuck."

She hated to admit that. More, she hated to admit it to Georgia, like maybe her secret wouldn't be safe any longer.

"Too bad," Georgia said. "Then what's your article about?"

"What article?"

"The one for *Flirt*? The magazine you're interning for? Wow, Elizabeth, you sound like such a flake."

"I'm not a flake." Elizabeth felt super-defensive. "I just haven't come up with an idea for an article yet." She turned to Georgia hopefully. The girl had traveled all over the world, met all sorts of people. She must have seen so many things, working in Hollywood since she was little. She probably had tons of ideas, and perhaps she'd be willing to share them? "Maybe we could brainstorm," she said. "Bounce ideas off each other . . ."

Georgia sniffed. "I already have my idea, I told you that."

"Oh."

She changed the subject. "What are you doing up on the roof, anyway?" She walked around to the other side of the chimney to find a beach umbrella and a giant lounge chair. A sheet was shrouding the umbrella to provide a private alcove around the chair. "Wow, what's this?" Elizabeth said. She started to approach the lounge chair.

"Don't!" Georgia shrieked. "That's mine. I spent hours setting it up."

Elizabeth took a step away. "Are you serious?"

"I need my space."

Elizabeth wanted to laugh. Georgia was too much.

Georgia wouldn't meet her eyes. She climbed into her lounge chair and started to close the sheet. "You know what? I need some privacy now. To think. Do you mind?"

"Not at all," Elizabeth said.

The sheet went down, hiding Georgia from view. All Elizabeth could see were her feet stretched out on the end of the lounger, clad in rhinestone-encrusted flip-flops.

From: cgack@gackliteraryagency.com
To: elizabeth_cheekwood@webdotmail.com
Re: Meeting this week

Elizabeth,

I'm thrilled to have you in New York, and we must take advantage. I know we discussed having the first draft of your novel ready by summer's end. I think it's time to meet to go over your progress. I only hope your internship isn't keeping you from your book!

How's Friday, lunch? You know how much I love your first three chapters, I've told you often enough. But now I want to see something new. Bring more!

Best,
Connie

chapter three

"**G**eorgia! Over here, Georgia!"

Georgia turned and another flashbulb went off in her face. She waved, she did a few poses, she signed a few shirts. One of the more enthusiastic photographers actually leaped in front of Georgia as she was about to enter the building. He shoved his camera in her face.

"Give Joey Joey a smile," the photographer said. Georgia had seen him before. He always talked about himself in the third person, like he was a star, too. The tie-dyed shirts he often wore made him easy to spot.

Georgia gave Joey Joey a smile, letting her dimples show. By the time she made it into the lobby of the Hudson-Bennett building, she was not just late for work, she was all by herself. The other interns had taken the elevator up without her.

Some friends, she thought. Her Hollywood friends would have stood by her, off to the side, ready to hold the door open when she was done with the cameras and wanted to go in. Of course, some of those friends had been on her payroll over the years—but still.

That was first thing in the morning. It was the Fourth of July, but a workday nonetheless. By mid-morning, the smattering of paparazzi had left the sidewalk outside the Hudson-Bennett building, and the streets of Times Square were now filled with cameras of another kind: those belonging to the tourists. The tourists used their cameras to snap one another. They snapped pix of the skyline, they snapped the yellow cabs, they got jostled in the crowd and accidentally snapped their shoes. There seemed to be even more tourists around, since it was a holiday. But they gave Georgia a moment of reprieve from the photos while she ran her errand, and she was thankful. Because Georgia Cooper of *Molly Mack* fame was now, for all intents and purposes, a simple intern of no fame whatsoever.

She was on an iced latte run for the Entertainment department's brainstorming session. Was she invited to brainstorm? No. Rather, she was asked to go out into the sticky early July heat—thicker and wetter than the heat she was used to in Southern California—to get other people loaded on caffeine. She put on a hat and huge, shaded sunglasses and went with head hung low to the closest Starbucks.

Be glad there's no paparazzi around to document this, she thought.

Back in the Hudson-Bennett lobby, she ran into an obstacle near the elevators. A guy about her age or a year or two older came through carrying a load of packages and a bicycle. She was carrying a tray of drinks and was trying to remove her sunglasses at the same time. Not a good idea. Georgia took a step this way, and the bicycle guy took a step that way, and the collision could have been messy. But the guy somehow took hold of her tray and the bike and his packages and miraculously, there was no spill.

"Thanks," Georgia breathed. She removed her sunglasses and slipped them into her pocket. Then she took back her tray.

They stepped onto the elevator together. Georgia fumbled over the wheel of his bike and righted herself against the elevator's sleek, mirrored wall. She pressed the button for the *Flirt* floor, and noticed that he didn't press any button.

He's going to my floor.

She turned away, acting totally uninterested. But at the same time, she observed him in the mirror. He had curly black hair just long enough to need a haircut; she liked that, the way he didn't care that he needed a haircut. He wore a T-shirt stretched taut over his shoulders and pants with one leg rolled up, for riding his bike through the city streets, probably. He had at least one visible tattoo. He had dark golden skin and—she tentatively lifted her gaze in the mirror to see—smoky hazel eyes.

"Hey," his image said to hers in the mirror.

She jumped and turned around. "Hi," she said back.

She waited for him to say what came next, what always came next. He'd ask, "Aren't you Molly Mack?" and she'd say, "As a matter of fact I am," and he'd say, "Would you do an autograph for my cousin/sister/friend? She's a big fan." And Georgia would say sure, and sign whatever he handed her, and that would be that.

But he didn't ask the question. They reached the *Flirt* floor and he moved the wheel of his bike so she could get off the elevator first. "Bye," he said.

"Bye," she echoed. She heard him at the reception desk, delivering packages. He was a bicycle messenger, the cutest bicycle messenger on Earth.

Back in the office, Georgia delivered the iced coffees to the Entertainment brainstorming session only to learn what had been brainstormed in her absence. The Entertainment department was only five editors and assistants, not including their intern. Without a department head—seeing as Ms. Bishop was still searching for someone to fill that job—they went around the table giving off ideas democratically. Georgia was hoping she'd get back with the coffees in time to give her own ideas, but the brainstorming seemed to be over and now they were on to the last-minute party planning.

> *He was a bicycle messenger, the cutest bicycle messenger on Earth.*

"Georgia, we decided that we'll need you at the Fourth of July party tonight," one of the Entertainment editors, Caitlain, said.

"Yeah, I'm going," Georgia said. "All the interns are."

"Not *going*," Caitlain said. "Working. Someone on the PR staff got food poisoning so we'll need you at the door, making sure whoever gets in is on the guest list. Mostly celebrities. Now, about the 'New Faces in Hollywood' section"—she turned to the rest of the Entertainment staff—"I say we add Ashley Tisdale."

Wait, what?! Did Caitlain just say they wanted her to WORK THE DOOR at a party, like a plebe?

She was having trouble breathing. She needed her stress coach. Or an herbal Valium.

"Excuse me," she said to the room. "I'll be right back."

No one batted an eye as she walked out of the conference room. She turned left—that was the way to the bathrooms, right? Maybe not. She changed her mind, turned right, and jetted around the corner too quickly, crashing into none other than the editor-in-chief of the whole shebang, Ms. Bishop.

"Is everything all right, Georgia?" Ms. Bishop asked. She seemed genuinely concerned.

"It's just about the party tonight, that's all," Georgia admitted.

"Ah," Ms. Bishop said. "You've learned that we need your help at the door."

She knew! She knew she was throwing me to the sidewalk wolves the whole time!

Georgia looked down at the floor. Ms. Bishop was wearing Ferragamo pumps—gorgeous.

Don't get distracted, Georgia told herself. "I thought you said all the interns were invited to attend the party. Not work at it. It's not fair."

Ms. Bishop smiled, seeming amused. "You're the Entertainment intern, Georgia, and the Entertainment department needs your help. I don't see anything unfair about that."

Georgia swallowed. She never should have said what she was really thinking in front of Ms. Bishop. That's why actors had *lines* to follow.

"As I recall from your impassioned application to this program, you are here to intern for the magazine, not be featured in it," Ms Bishop said. "Is that still the case?"

"Yes," Georgia said, but more quietly than she meant to.

"Good," Ms. Bishop said. "I think tonight will be a fine experience for you. It will show you a whole new side to the world of celebrities, now won't it?"

"Yes," Georgia said. She had never been so submissive in her whole entire life. *Stop!* she told herself. *Be assertive. Be the star, not the walk-on extra!* "But I'm also hoping, this summer, to have some of my writing featured in the magazine. It's why I'm here, after all. To be a writer."

Ms. Bishop had been about to walk away, but she turned back to Georgia, seeming surprised. "I didn't know that you considered yourself a writer, Georgia."

"I do," Georgia said. "I'm giving up acting to be a writer."

Maybe not giving it up . . . *but definitely taking a break for a while.*

"I see," Ms. Bishop said. Her face was unreadable. "Wear good shoes tonight, Georgia. You'll be spending a lot of time on your feet." At that, she glided away on her stunning Ferragamos.

Georgia felt both relieved and embarrassed. She'd just confided in Ms. Bishop that she was giving up acting; she never thought she'd say that out loud. She wanted Ms. Bishop to think of her as the writer of the group.

Except, of course, Elizabeth already was the writer of the group.

I bet she *doesn't have to work the door at the party,* Georgia thought stormily.

☉　　☉　　☉　　☉

Sure enough, there was one intern working the door, and one intern only. Usually Georgia was the one gliding through the velvet rope, saying her name was on "the list." Now she was running her finger down the list trying to find the names. It was agony.

The *Flirt*-sponsored party was on a floating barge toward the southeastern end of Manhattan island. Limos abounded. Celebrities wore all white. Entourages were in full effect. The holiday fireworks were set to go off over the water in mere minutes. And there stood Georgia, on the wrong side of the velvet rope, guarding the entrance. All the other interns were inside. Nova had even flaunted the rules and snuck a friend in—ignoring the fact that Ms. Bishop had explicitly said that interns could not bring guests.

Nova doesn't think the rules apply to her, Georgia thought. *If anyone should get special treatment, it's me. Tell me why I'm slaving out here about to miss the fireworks?*

"Georgia!" one of the public relations girls said. "I thought you were here to help!" She had headphones on and clipboard in hand, and her no-excuses attitude with the party crashers was a learning experience in itself. Now she had her steely eyes on Georgia, who had snuck out of the fray to sit down on the curb.

Georgia stretched out a leg to show off her Prada heels. "It's just these shoes are killing me and I didn't know I'd have to stand here all night and, hey, when can we go inside, anyway?" She'd worn the heels to match the all black outfit she had been asked to wear, but her blacks involved a Tom Ford skirt and sleek beaded top from Miu

> ## "She tried a pout, but the PR girl wasn't having it."

Miu. She wanted to look good for any run-ins with the paparazzi, not that it mattered, seeing as all they cared about was chasing down shots of Kanye and Mischa and, hey, was that Orlando Bloom?

The PR girl rolled her eyes at Georgia and then turned to one of her coworkers, another girl in all black. "I told you," she hissed. Then to Georgia she said, "I take it you're asking for a break."

Georgia nodded. She tried a pout, but the PR girl wasn't having it.

"Fifteen minutes," the PR girl said. "And you really should have worn more practical shoes."

Georgia leaped up from the curb—forgetting the probable blisters on her heels from the strappy shoes now that she got to leave her post. She had fifteen minutes and fifteen minutes only. She'd better make them good.

She swept into the party. It was just as she'd imagined, just like the hot invite-only parties she was used to attending on the coasts, except this time she wasn't even really invited. She was embarrassed about having to work the door, to sign in Tara and Paris and Nicole (separately, of course) and have them recognize her and say the things she knew they would say once she was out of sight.

It was cruel and unusual punishment.

Georgia kept to the sidelines. Very Important People, as well as their hangers-on, crowded the floating room. Lights sparkled on the tables and on the railings overlooking the water. When the fireworks went off, it would be like they were shrieking and fizzing and exploding in awesome bangs of noise and color only for them.

She was about to check the clock on her cell to see how much time she had left before the PR girls out front hit her over the head with their clipboards and dragged her back out front. But then she saw something even more disturbing than a B-list celebrity getting wasted enough to think she merited the attention of an A. Georgia had spotted two of her fellow interns—Mikki and (guess who?) Elizabeth—hamming it up on the dance floor. Mikki had an ease about her; it was clear she liked to dance and she was good at it. But Elizabeth was a train wreck in a glitterati dress that was clearly borrowed, because the shoulder straps couldn't stay up. She did a rabid twirl that looked like a cross between a drunk ballerina and a crunked-out clown.

"That's beautiful," Georgia said aloud. Elizabeth was making a fool of herself. Just wait till Ms. Bishop saw this. Her star writer would fall, and fast. Georgia had to stay to see what happened. Besides, there were three of the other interns—Sivya and Asha and Nailah, waving her over to a spot near the railing. Then *bang, crack, bang*—

the fireworks were going off overhead. No way was Georgia leaving the party now.

᧥ ᧥ ᧥ ᧥

stalkerazzi.com

Currently stalking . . . Georgia Cooper . . . spotted at *Flirt* mag's 4th of July bash, lounging out under the fireworks like the megastar she thinks she still is. Rumor has it she ditched her oh-so-glamorous job of guarding the door for the glitz and glam of the party's inner sanctum. We hear tell her new boss, Queen Bishop, was none too happy and is about to crack her (Prada, black leather, $13,500) whip! Way to make a good impression your first week on the job, Georgie Girl. Hope Bishop doesn't send you packing back to the Hills. But if you want to stay in NYC, check with us. We're always looking for new ~~slaves~~ interns. Besides, you still owe us that latte!

᧥ ᧥ ᧥ ᧥

"Explain what happened," Ms. Bishop said. "I would like to hear it, Georgia."

Georgia was sitting in a sleek white chair across the sleek white desk from Ms. Bishop. Ms. Bishop, it seemed, had caught sight of Georgia living it up at the party but had—by some cruel slip of fate—missed the floor show Elizabeth had given.

Why isn't Elizabeth in here getting a talking-to? Georgia thought.

Still, she couldn't help but be completely and totally freaked out by the look of utter seriousness on Ms. Bishop's face.

"Well?" Ms. Bishop said. "Why did you think you could stop working when you felt like it?"

Because it was a party and, hello, I wanted to have fun.

Because my feet hurt.

Because what if my ex, Anton Stone, showed up with whoever his new girlfriend is now and I had to sign them both in?

Because it wasn't fair. Isn't that reason enough?

Georgia couldn't say any of that. She realized how it must have looked to everyone. She looked like a slacker. She looked like a vapid celebrity who just didn't care about the magazine or her internship. And that wasn't true—Georgia loved the magazine. No one could ever doubt that.

Truth is, she'd really messed up. No excuses.

"I am so very sorry," Georgia said, channeling

some especially mature role she never had: young defense lawyer, yeah, or better yet, repentant criminal. She sat up straight; she looked Ms. Bishop in the eyes; she made sure her voice didn't waver. "I owe you an apology," she said. "I acted immature and irresponsible. I should have stayed at my post. I won't do anything like that again."

She waited for Ms. Bishop's response.

Man, that sounded solid. No way could she stay mad now.

Ms. Bishop, however, was not responding. She was waiting as well, as if Georgia should be saying something else.

Line! Line! Georgia wanted to yell out. *What's my next line?!*

Finally, she just said, "Please, Ms. Bishop. Please don't send me home."

"Don't be overdramatic, Georgia. I wasn't happy with your behavior last night, but you're not here this summer to guard doors. Now, is it true you want to write?"

"Oh, yes. That's my dream. I want to write an article for *Flirt*. I want to be in the 'New Faces' issue." She felt shy.

66 *I owe you an apology. I acted immature and irresponsible. I should have stayed at my post. I won't do anything like that again.* **99**

> **66** *I know I asked you to come up with ideas for your own story, but since I have this one open, I thought I'd try you on it. With your unique perspective on Hollywood, it could be the perfect fit.* **99**

"If I do something good enough, that is," she added.

"I hope you will," Ms. Bishop said. Then she handed Georgia a red folder. A name was clipped to the front: Eve Bridges. "I know I asked you to come up with ideas for your own story, but since I have this one open, I thought I'd try you on it. With your unique perspective on Hollywood, it could be the perfect fit."

Georgia glanced inside the folder. Eve was a young actress, sixteen, Georgia's age. She'd been in one movie and had a recurring role on one daytime soap. Nothing that impressive. "So an interview?" Georgia said. "Talk to her about her personal history, her childhood, her plans for her career, her future, her greatest fears, her—"

"Don't go overboard. It's a small profile. You'll have at most two hundred words. Eve expects to meet a representative from the magazine today at three o'clock. Surely you two have enough in common to have a nice chat. Interested?"

"Yes!" Georgia practically shouted. "I'm definitely

interested." She was going to produce the most smokin' two hundred words Ms. Bishop had ever seen.

"Good," Ms. Bishop said. Then she swiveled on her sleek swivel chair to face her computer and Georgia took that as a hint to leave.

Saved, Georgia thought. *Saved by a soap star.*

Still, once safe in her own cubicle, Georgia breathed a long, heavy sigh of gut-wrenching, soul-cleansing relief.

I messed up, she admitted to herself. *And Ms. Bishop still wants me to stay.*

◉   ◉   ◉   ◉

"So what made you decide to be an actress?" Georgia asked Eve Bridges, reading from the list of questions in her steno book. They sat in Caffe Pane in the Village, with Eve in sunglasses even though the inside of the café was dimly lit. The girl obviously thought she was a superstar. It was pathetic. Georgia was doing all she could to keep to her list of questions and not laugh in Eve's face.

Eve sighed. "I was in drama club. I went on auditions, yadda yadda, don't you have any *deeper* questions?"

Georgia skimmed her list. "What interested you about acting in soaps?"

Eve sighed again, adjusting her sunglasses. "Can we smoke in here? You make me want a cigarette."

"No, you *cannot* smoke in here," Georgia said. *Ick.*

"" Can we smoke in here? You make me want a cigarette. ""

The girl was egotistical and gross. "So tell me about acting on the soap," she said, looking into the dark, solid squares of Eve's sunglasses. It was hard to interview a person without being able to see her eyes.

"I've seen your show, you know," Eve said.

Georgia put on her camera-ready smile. So the girl was a nasty smoker and a bigheaded diva, but she was also a fan. Beautiful. "Really," she said.

"You were so good when you were young," Eve said. "What happened?"

"What do you mean what happened? I starred in a top-rated TV show for five years. It had its run, and it was a great run, and now it's over. That's what happened."

"I don't mean what happened to the show. I mean what happened to *you*?"

Georgia narrowed her eyes. "Nothing happened to me. I'm right here."

"Exactly. You're here interviewing a star instead of being the star. It's—what's the word . . . ?"

"Ironic," Georgia said in a flat voice. She wanted to reach across the teeny-tiny table and strangle Eve Bridges. Or else pour the ice-cold tea on Eve's lap.

But how would Ms. Bishop react to that? Georgia thought. *No, I have to be mature. I have to do my job.*

She consulted her list of questions. They were stupid. She hated it when journalists asked her dumb, boring questions like these. This article was going to suck. And Eve knew it.

Is she trying to be even more boring to make sure it sucks?

Georgia had to go on the fly. She picked a question out of thin air. "So, Eve, tell me . . . do you think that acting on the soap opera tainted your career and ruined you for any solid roles? Do you consider it a huge mistake?"

"What? No," Eve said. "Of course not."

"Is that so," Georgia said, jotting down a note on her steno pad. *Gotcha.*

"In fact," Eve said, "I always knew that the soap was just the start for me. TV was temporary. Now that I've broken through with my first big-screen role, I expect a long-lasting career in movies. I won't let my career dry up, like some people."

Is she talking about me? Oh, she is SO not talking about me.

Georgia balled up her fists. She balled up her toes. She got ready to throw a few good, solid insults at the pathetic little soap actress before her and then . . .

She stopped. She steeled herself not to react. Some things were just more important.

Georgia returned to her list of boring, safe questions. "So what was it like working with Owen Wilson? He's funny, huh?"

◎　　◎　　◎　　◎

Georgia was getting off the elevator back at the *Flirt* office as the bicycle messenger was trying to get on. There was a bit of a struggle. Georgia tried to get past him, but the gigantic wheel of his bike was in the way.

"Could you please . . . move?!" Georgia burst out. She didn't mean to be rude, but the whole Eve Bridges interview had her feeling all touchy.

"Sorry," the bike messenger guy said. He looked, oh, disappointed in her? Like he expected her to be better than she was. He lifted the bike so she could get past.

She turned. "God, I'm so sorry. I'm just having a sucky day."

"Not a problem," he said, shrugging.

"I'm Georgia," she said, stating the obvious. "And you are . . . ?"

"Tyler," he said. "We've been running into each other a lot lately. It's nice to put a name to a face."

Does he really not know who I am? she thought. *That's so . . . annoying!*

No, strike that. Not annoying. Refreshing.

She smiled. It was her real-life smile, not her on-

❝God, I'm so sorry. I'm just having a sucky day.❞

camera smile. Not that he'd know the difference. "See you around, Tyler. I promise not to be so nasty next time."

"I'll hold you to that," he said.

Then they went their separate ways. She had a story to write. She had to find two hundred words of genius from a two-hour interview of grade-A blech.

Help!

chapter four

"So Monday, then," Elizabeth's literary agent, Constance Gack, said. "I assume that won't be a problem?"

"No problem," Elizabeth assured her. And it was true: At that moment, over a Friday afternoon lunch at Nico's, a luxurious restaurant close to the Hudson-Bennett building, the Monday deadline seemed entirely possible. Elizabeth wasn't the least bit concerned, even keeping in mind that she had another deadline that same day, and this one for the magazine. Ms. Bishop had scheduled a Monday morning meeting with all the interns to pitch their pieces for the "New Faces" issue.

Constance Gack, the literary agent known for taking huge risks with unknown authors—and also for representing a few very high-profile celebrity authors, thus making it more possible to take such risks—was actually sitting across the table from Elizabeth for the first time. They had only before spoken on the phone, or through e-mail. Elizabeth was humbled. This woman—close-cropped steel gray hair, black eyes like laser pointers—was here to help Elizabeth. She thought Elizabeth was a good writer. She loved the first three chapters of her novel and was now dying to see more. She said she was going to make Elizabeth famous.

"Elizabeth," Ms. Gack was saying, "please, I need you to tell me if this is too much. Are you under a lot of pressure with your internship?"

"No, not at all," Elizabeth said. "It's fun." She avoided Ms. Gack's probing eyes.

Ms. Gack had wanted her to bring her latest chapters to their lunch meeting—she'd e-mailed twice to say how excited she was to read them. She said she had a publishing house lined up to take a first look. It was all so thrilling, so surreal—until Elizabeth had walked into Nico's without the pages. She'd said she just hadn't had a chance to print them out, and Ms. Gack had seemed terribly disappointed, so much so that Elizabeth felt slightly guilty about lying, but she'd kept going with it.

"I can e-mail them to you tonight?" she found herself saying. To herself, thinking: *Maybe the e-mail won't go through? Not all e-mails get to their destination a hundred percent of the time. I heard that . . . somewhere.*

"Oh no, that won't work," Ms. Gack said. "I'll be on Fire Island this weekend. It will have to be Monday."

And so Elizabeth was saddled with not one but two deadlines on Monday, her novel and her article, both of equal importance, and both—to admit the truth—not done.

Elizabeth was paying special attention to her pasta primavera. She stabbed a broccoli spear, held it aloft, inspected it, took a nibble, turned it over, inspected it again—

❝ *Oh no, that won't work. I'll be on Fire Island this weekend. It will have to be Monday.* **❞**

"So, Elizabeth, tell me how many new chapters you have ready," Ms. Gack said.

Elizabeth put down the broccoli. "Three more," she lied.

"Fabulous," Ms. Gack said with great enthusiasm.

Three more? Three! Why did I say that?!

But the lies kept coming. "I think you'll like them, Connie, I mean Ms. Gack."

What?! I haven't written them yet. Shut up.

Elizabeth shoved the whole piece of broccoli in her mouth: a safety measure. That way, she couldn't keep talking.

"Please, call me Connie," Ms. Gack said. "I insist. I'm looking forward to reading your new chapters. As is the editor I told you about. If she likes them, she might even make a preemptive offer. Wouldn't that be fabulous?"

"Fabulous," Elizabeth repeated. Then she nodded and smiled. No more lies slipped out when she kept her mouth closed.

She swallowed her last bit of broccoli and just hoped none of it was stuck to her teeth. The plates were cleared and Ms. Gack—Connie—was shaking her hand, quite pleased. Elizabeth was about to wrestle her purse strap off the back of her chair when she heard her name.

"Ah look, it's Elizabeth Cheekwood! She's my new Features intern. Elizabeth, this is Kate Spade; Kate, Elizabeth. And Connie, it's wonderful to see you again—"

"Jo, you never did tell me—how was St. Barts?"

Elizabeth stood there, the conversation of glamorous trips and glamorous people far over her head. Within minutes, the group was out on the sidewalk saying their good-byes, and Elizabeth was walking back to the Hudson-Bennett building with Ms. Bishop as if they'd just come from a private lunch together.

On the elevator, Ms. Bishop turned to Elizabeth. "Tell me about the progress of your article," Ms. Bishop said.

Don't lie, Elizabeth admonished herself.

But she obviously couldn't listen to herself because as she glided through the glass doors of the *Flirt* offices and down the corridors at Ms. Bishop's side, she found herself saying, "The article is going great! I can't wait for you to read it!"

Ms. Bishop said she was looking forward to it. And then she said, "I do hope there's not too much pressure on you this summer. I know Connie has you working hard on your novel. Are you having any problems juggling your book and your internship?"

"Oh, no. No problems," Elizabeth assured Ms. Bishop.

"All right, then," Ms. Bishop said. "Have a good weekend." They parted ways in the corridor and Elizabeth headed to her cubicle, ignoring the alarm bells in her head.

She collided with Georgia, who had another scowl on her face. "Did you and Ms. Bishop just come back from lunch together?" Georgia asked coldly.

"Yeah, we were at Nico's and—"

"Nico's," Georgia repeated. "You and Ms. Bishop were just at Nico's."

"We—"

Georgia put her hand in front of Elizabeth's face. "Don't say another word. I don't want to hear it."

She turned on her heel and stomped off in the opposite direction. "Beautiful," Elizabeth heard Georgia mutter as she walked away. "She takes her to Nico's."

"Not together!" Elizabeth called out, but it was too late. Georgia had made a swift turn down another corridor and out of sight.

❧   ❧   ❧   ❧

Friday night, Elizabeth wrote two sentences, one for each project:

1) *I can't write this article right now because I don't feel like it.*

2) *I can't write this book right now because I don't feel like it.*

She was stuck, times two. Then she erased both sentences and went to hang out with the girls in the living room. Soon enough, the night was nearly over and she told herself she'd do a ton of writing in the morning. She had the whole weekend, after all.

But when Saturday morning rolled around, Mikki had an idea. "A tour of New York City! Oh, Nova, you have to take us!"

"I don't have to do anything," Nova said. She was picking at a sourdough bagel and sipping coffee at the breakfast table.

"But you were born here," Sivya put in. "You know the city better than any of us. And this is the first time Asha, Mikki, and Nailah have ever been to New York, ever. You don't want us getting lost on the way to South Ferry and ending up in the Bronx, do you?"

"That wouldn't happen," Nova said. "They're in completely opposite directions."

"See?!" Mikki said. "How are we supposed to know? Mate, you've got to be our tour guide."

Sivya gave a goofy grin. "Pleeeeeeeeeeeaaaaase?"

Nova grabbed a napkin and drew a map of Manhattan. On the bottom it said SOUTH FERRY. On the top there was an arrow that said TO THE BRONX. "There," she said, shoving it over to Sivya. "You guys go. There's no way I'm touring the Statue of Liberty—I've been up to the top of that thing, like, fifty times."

"I second that," Georgia called from the kitchen. "The Statue of Liberty—snore." Nailah had just made a juice smoothie for herself and one for Georgia. Georgia had a way of getting people to do things for her, one of her many talents.

Elizabeth was sitting on the couch, listening in. She was hoping for some sudden inspiration, like a shot of lightning through the roof of the building. She had her laptop by her side, waiting for it. Nothing came.

"Not the Statue of Liberty, then," Sivya said. "Blindfold us. Put bags over our heads and spin us around ten times. Then take us to all your top secret hot spots and we won't be able to give them away because we won't even know how to get there!"

"I don't know about bags over our heads, but a tour would rock," Mikki said. "I've decided. I'm going, and

❝ There's no way I'm touring the Statue of Liberty—I've been up to the top of that thing, like, fifty times. ❞

whoever wants to come with can come with." She had that contagious light in her eyes. Mikki was just so much fun—no one could deny it.

"I do have chemistry homework . . ." Asha said. "But I'll go with you, Mikki." She shrugged. "I bet it will be fun."

"Mikki, I'll go," Nailah added.

Mikki turned to Elizabeth. "Lizzy?"

Elizabeth had been up to the top of the Statue of Liberty before, with her parents. "I don't know," she said. "I have so much work to do."

"Fine," Nova said suddenly. But she was smiling. "You've talked me into it, Mikki. If you guys want a tour, I'll give you a tour. But not to any tourist traps."

Mikki looked about to bounce off the walls. "Where are we going?" she asked.

"It'll be a fashion tour. So wear your walking shoes. I'm getting changed." At that, Nova swept upstairs, leaving Mikki leaping around the kitchen in ecstatic happiness. The delirium was catching and, within minutes, even Nailah and Asha were acting excited. Only Elizabeth and Georgia were left unscathed.

Except, Elizabeth sort of wanted to drop her laptop and go on the tour, too.

"Lizzy, you *have to* come," Mikki said, grinning.

"What Mikki said. You have to," Sivya added.

Elizabeth was just about to relent—saying she

> ## It was alarming how quickly her mood had shifted.

could work on her writing later that night—when Georgia butted in.

"Like *I* don't have work to do," she said. "Like we all don't?" She was talking to Elizabeth, her eyes blazing.

Why does she seem so mad? Elizabeth thought, truly confused. "But my agent wants to see my novel—" she started.

"So what?" Georgia said.

"And when Ms. Bishop and I were walking back from Nico's she told me she's expecting something really good from me on Monday. She said she was excited to read it and . . ." her voice trailed off. She hadn't meant to brag.

"Wow," Sivya breathed.

"I know!" Georgia grumbled.

"I mean, I didn't know Ms. Bishop *walked*. You'd think she'd have a private helicopter to take her down the block."

Mikki laughed.

Georgia turned back to Elizabeth. But her expression had softened. It was alarming how quickly her mood had shifted. "Lizzy," she said, "you know what I think? I think you do deserve a break. You work sooooooo hard. It's not fair. This is your first weekend in New York. You've got to come on the tour! Don't you think so, girls?"

"Yeah, mate," Mikki said, grinning.

"Uh-huh," Asha said. "If I'm stopping my chem homework to go, you're going also. What do you say?"

"All right," Elizabeth said. She was flattered that they cared enough to convince her.

Plus, she was relieved. Who wanted to sit hunched over a hot laptop all day when she could go on a fashion tour of New York City?

ⓖ   ⓖ   ⓖ   ⓖ

Nova started the tour in SoHo, their very own neighborhood, leading the girls through the artists' tables on Prince Street and Spring Street, where she said they could find the best handmade jewelry and hats and hand-painted T-shirts. Mikki was on cloud nine, ten, and whatever came next—so completely inspired, Elizabeth couldn't help but be inspired along with her. Nailah bought a hat and Sivya bought a shirt (black and gray—her usual color scheme). Nova shuttled the girls through the smaller designer boutiques in the neighborhood, and they were only delayed by photographers twice, once when Georgia removed her sunglasses to try on some designer knockoffs, which she of course didn't purchase, and a second time outside the Betsey Johnson boutique, where a small group of photographers seemed to be waiting for her and then followed the girls, snapping pictures, until they escaped onto the subway.

"Now the Upper East Side," Nova announced. She appeared to be having fun for the first time, and she hadn't even asked her city friends to go along.

The girls walked Madison Avenue, going into the fanciest stores, even though no one but Georgia could afford to buy from them.

"I just like to look," Nova explained. "It gives me ideas."

"I have an idea," Sivya said as they peeked at the evening gowns in Prada. "I'm going to try this one on." She held up a midnight blue gown with intricate beading along the bodice. It had thin, microscopic straps. It looked so delicate, Elizabeth wouldn't have wanted to touch it without wearing gloves.

Sivya gazed at it. "Could you imagine me in this?"

"Actually . . ." Asha said. "Being honest? No."

True, it was an example in contrasts. There was Sivya in her frayed black jeans with the hole in the back pocket and the hole in the knee, with the wallet chain hanging out. She wore a black T-shirt and black skateboarding sneakers. She dressed like a boy.

But Georgia was nodding. "I have got to see this," she said. "Sivya, try it on."

Sivya looked to Mikki for approval. "I say go for it," Mikki said.

"Then I will," Sivya said. She dragged the gown toward the dressing room. It was then that the salesgirl came out on full alert.

"Oh, no," she said, leaping at Sivya like a linebacker. "That's not necessary."

"I can't try it on?" Sivya asked.

"Are you planning on purchasing it?" the salesgirl asked icily. She was a walking Prada ad, all tight hair, big eyes, smoky outfit, and silk-sheathed legs. By the way she looked down her nose at Sivya, it was clear she'd never walked out of the house with a gaping hole in the knee of her pants, not once.

"I doubt I could afford it," Sivya said, so unbearably honest, "but I just thought maybe I could—"

The salesgirl took the gown from Sivya's hands. "I'd rather you not try it on, then," she said.

Nova reached out and peeked at the price tag on the dress. Elizabeth saw her try to keep the shock from her face. "Sivya, it's really not that much. I'm sure you could talk your parents into it. For prom."

"Prom?" Sivya said, dumbfounded.

"Prom shopping, in the *summer*?" the salesgirl said, her smile almost a snarl.

"She likes to think ahead," Nova said.

The salesgirl walked the gown

❝She was a walking Prada ad.❞

back to the rack. "Feel free to come back with your parents."

"Why can't my friend try it on if she wants to? She's not going to rip off a strap or something," Nova said, now getting all riled up. It was more emotion than Elizabeth had seen in the girl since she met her—apparently Nova did not like to be told no.

"I'd rather she didn't," the salesgirl said with a sniff, all haughty attitude as she smoothed the gown back in place on the rack.

Elizabeth looked from Nova to Sivya to the salesgirl, and back to Nova, who looked about to start throwing the Prada summer collection onto the floor.

Are we really going to cause a scene? Elizabeth thought. *Over some ridiculous dress Sivya would never wear anyway, even if she could afford it?*

"I don't need to try it on, Nova, really," Sivya said quietly.

"Yeah, let's go," Elizabeth said.

Suddenly Georgia stepped forward, an expression on her face that Elizabeth recognized from her TV show. It was the you're-going-to-do-what-I-want-and-you're-going-to-like-it expression, which the girl detective Molly Mack would use on reluctant witnesses and anyone else who got in her way. It was so sweet, and yet so unbudging, that most characters on her show stopped any argument at that point and said, "Sure, Miss Mack, take a look through my closet—I don't mind."

Georgia settled the expression on the salesgirl and said, "She won't take long. Ten minutes tops. You won't even notice we're here." She held out a hand for the dress.

Georgia's going to get us kicked out, Elizabeth realized. She took an involuntarily step toward the door. Nailah and Asha were close behind.

But the salesgirl shifted gears quicker than it took for Elizabeth to blink. She gasped. "You're Georgia Cooper!" she said.

Georgia smiled the fakest smile this side of the Atlantic. "That I am."

"I didn't recognize you," the salesgirl said. "I'm so sorry. I didn't mean to be rude to your friend." And like a dream—or some scene on TV—the salesgirl was retrieving the blue dress from the rack and holding it out to Sivya, and Sivya was in the dressing room trying it on, and Mikki was snapping photos with her mini digital, and Sivya was saying, "Huh, maybe I should get dressed up more often," and everyone was laughing at how elegant she looked in the gorgeous beaded creation with her sneakers on. The girls left the store without buying a thing.

Out on the sidewalk, Sivya hugged Georgia like she'd just given her a kidney.

"Thanks, Georgia. That was fun. And so weird to look like a girl for once!"

"You know, if you want to look like a girl more often, I'll buy it for you," Georgia said. "No big."

"No way," Sivya said.

Georgia shrugged. "I'm just saying."

"Yeah, Georgia, that was nice of you," Asha said.

"I said it was no big." She turned and made a point of looking at Elizabeth. "I just don't like it when things are unfair."

Why is she looking at me? Elizabeth thought.

"See, Georgia?" Nova said. "The diva act can really come in handy."

"I am *not* a diva," Georgia said, her face getting all pinched.

"No?" Nova said lightly. It wasn't clear if she was teasing or not.

Please don't let the two of them get into a fight out here in the middle of Madison Avenue, Elizabeth thought, fearing the worst. There was something about Georgia she just didn't trust—like whatever she did was always first for her own benefit, second still for her benefit, and third, maybe then for someone else.

But Georgia shrugged, a small smile on her face. "Hey, you do what you have to do, am I right?"

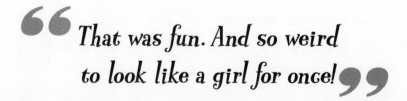

That was fun. And so weird to look like a girl for once!

"So right," Nova said, like they'd reached some sort of understanding.

Asha glanced at Elizabeth and shrugged. Mikki rolled her eyes, and Nailah just shook her head, smiling. Then they all kept going down Madison Avenue, looking for some more fancy-schmancy stores to terrorize.

ᚼ   ᚼ   ᚼ   ᚼ

Nova's fashion tour of New York led them back downtown, to the finale, as she called it: the secondhand stores, flea markets, and consignment shops where she got her best fashion finds, many of which were then torn apart and reconstructed, like the netted denim skirt she wore now. The girls traipsed through the Lower East Side and Nolita and the East Village and then collapsed in a shopping stupor on the benches of Tompkins Square Park. They sucked on asai smoothies, made from a Brazilian berry known for giving immense energy boosts, better even than a Venti cup from the coffee chain across the street. Shopping bags were piled up at their feet.

Even Nailah was drinking an asai smoothie—it was filled with antioxidants, she said. Elizabeth sipped at hers (so strong, it made her head spin). She knew she needed to come up with some brilliant idea for her *Flirt* article so she could pitch it at the meeting on Monday and blow everyone, specifically Ms. Bishop, away. Plus, she needed to write some more brilliant chapters for her novel . . . no pressure on both fronts, ha. But for the moment, she just couldn't move from her spot on the bench.

"I'm beat," Nova said, sharing the bench with Elizabeth. "This asai better kick in soon, or else I'll crash right here before Jessica and Kate get here."

"Who are Jessica and Kate?" Elizabeth asked lazily.

"There they are," Nova said, leaping up and leaving Elizabeth on the bench by herself.

"Did you know she was hanging out with her friends tonight?" Sivya asked Elizabeth. She took Nova's seat on the bench.

"No . . ." Elizabeth said. "But she always hangs out with her friends."

Nova approached the interns with her two friends in tow. "So we're gonna take off," she said.

Mikki stood up. "What!? Where are you mates going? The tour's not over, is it?"

> **She needed to write some more brilliant chapters for her novel.**

Nova laughed. "The tour guide is going out"—she glanced at her friends, who seemed impatient to leave the park—"someplace crazy."

"I wish," one of her friends said, either Jessica or Kate. "If only Raffi was here."

"Who's Raffi?" Mikki said.

"Raffi goes to our school," Nova said. "He always knows the most insane places to check out. We'd be so utterly bored without him."

"He's a freak," one of her friends said, apparently a high compliment.

"We'll just have to make do without him," the other said. "So are we out?"

"Yeah," Nova said, then she turned back as if in an afterthought. "Whoever wants to can come with." She left the invite hanging there, and Elizabeth shocked even herself by bursting out before Nova could leave:

"I'm in."

Nova turned back, raising an eyebrow. "Yeah?" she said. "It'll be a late night."

"Definitely," Elizabeth said.

"Me too," Mikki said. "Late is good."

"Um," Asha piped up. "What about curfew? Anyway, I'm going back to the loft. My feet hurt—I think I'll get a taxi."

"I'm with you," Sivya said. "I've had enough excitement for one day."

"Good, then you can take our bags," Mikki said, shoving her shopping finds at Asha and Sivya.

The interns split into two groups: the homebodies—Asha, Sivya, and Nailah—and those not afraid of breaking curfew—Nova, Mikki, and none other than Elizabeth, surprised to find herself standing on the side she was on.

Still undecided was Georgia. "You sure you have the time?" she said to Elizabeth.

What, is she my babysitter now? Elizabeth thought.

"Going someplace crazy will inspire me," she said. "I hope."

"If Lizzy has the time, then I have the time," Georgia said. "Who cares about curfew, right, Lizzy?"

"Yeah," Elizabeth said. A stranger had taken over her body. "Who cares?"

◉   ◉   ◉   ◉

Someone cared about curfew. Someone cared very much. Emma was so not pleased when Nova, Elizabeth, Mikki, and Georgia were almost two hours late, she was about to spit fire. They were banned from going out on Sunday, and Ms. Bishop would hear about this come Monday. Elizabeth felt stung—she'd never, ever gotten yelled at before by an authority figure—but she was also relieved. She needed to stay in on Sunday and work on her two projects. She needed inspiration! Motivation!

First, though, she needed sleep.

And sleep she did. So deeply, and for so long, that she could have kept sleeping if the phone hadn't been for her. It was her mom.

It took Elizabeth a full five minutes to understand

what her mom was talking about. "How are you, honey? How have you been managing your time? Did that calendar software I gave you help?"

"The calendar, yeah," Elizabeth said. Truth: She hadn't even opened it.

"You must be working very hard," her mom said. "I'm so proud of you. So, what did you do last night?"

"I stayed in, just worked on my article, you know." *I'm lying to my parents now—and it's so much easier than I thought.*

Her mom kept talking. She was planning to visit New York soon and wanted to see Elizabeth's office. She'd also had a good chat with Constance Gack and was thrilled to hear that the novel was moving along so smoothly. Apparently, Elizabeth's mom thought she was perfectly on top of things and in no trouble at all. Elizabeth let her keep thinking it. She talked to her dad for a while, too, letting him think the same thing, and then got off the phone and lazily wandered downstairs.

"I have so much to do!" she told Asha, who was calmly putting aside her finished chemistry homework to work on her pitch for the "New Faces" issue.

"Then you shouldn't have stayed out last night," Asha said in a measured voice. She was trying not to be judgmental, Elizabeth could tell.

"I know!" Elizabeth wailed. "But it's too late now."

Nailah came over, putting some sour-smelling tea

> ## **I'm lying to my parents now— and it's so much easier than I thought.**

on the table before her. "You need to calm down. Try this—it's herbal."

Elizabeth took a sip. "Thanks," she said. "You guys are the best."

"So," Asha said, "how crazy was it last night?"

Elizabeth recalled a whirlwind of clubs and a late after-party underground in what may have been a subway tunnel. It was crazier than anything she'd ever done, that was for sure. But she didn't want anyone thinking she was a wimp. "It was okay," she said.

"Drink that tea," Asha said. "Wait there—I'm going to get my rejuvenation eye mask. I put it together last night. It'll get you inspired, I know it."

"Okay," Elizabeth said. She sat at the table. She wrote an e-mail to Melanie Henderson, the previous Features intern, just saying hi, and maybe asking for a little advice. It took practically all her energy to write the thing.

Her laptop was still before her. She opened the new chapters of her novel. So far, only a single word was typed in. She looked at the word, but the letters started swimming. Seconds later, her eyes were closing, and her head was on her laptop, and she was out before the tea had a chance to calm her, before the mask had a chance to rejuvenate her, before she could squeeze out even one more word.

The

From: melwrites247@freemail.com
To: elizabeth_cheekwood@webdotmail.com
Subject: Re: Writer's block, help!

Hi, Elizabeth!

I just want to say it's really cool that my experience as the Features intern last summer has been helpful. But about your e-mail, it sucks you have writer's block, and believe me, I, too, have wanted to dunk my head in a bowl of ice water to get the ideas flowing. (Doubt that would work, though; what about brain freeze?) The best advice I can give is to do what you can for Monday. You really can't go into a meeting with Ms. Bishop unprepared—that's like death to an intern. Come up with something! Anything!

I'm totally sorry this e-mail is so rushed, but I didn't want to leave you without an answer. Right now my boyfriend is taking me out to some surprise place and he won't even tell me if I should dress up or not! You probably heard about my boyfriend, Emma's son, Nick? I met him when I was an intern and . . . well, one thing led to another and now here I am visiting him in Rome! So I can promise you one thing: Your life will never be the same after this summer. You can't know what will change, or how, but it so will.

Now go work really hard and brainstorm like crazy and I know Ms. Bishop will love you Monday morning. No doubt.

Hugs even though I don't know you (yet!),
Mel

ⓖ　ⓖ　ⓖ　ⓖ

It was so late Sunday night, it was practically morning. Elizabeth had fallen asleep at her laptop, facedown on the keys. She stumbled into the bathroom, splashed water on her face, and paused, staring at herself in the mirror. *What am I going to do?*

First, her agent, Constance Gack: *Say I need another week to polish. Good one. She'll never guess.*

Then Ms. Bishop . . . At the pitch meeting, Elizabeth would have to say something. Anything.

"An idea will come. Maybe if I sleep on it."

"Talking to yourself, are you?" a voice said.

Caught, Elizabeth whirled around to find a friendly face. It was Mikki, a big glob of bright green paint stuck to her hair. Elizabeth grinned. "Omigod, what did you do?"

> **"Who would have writer's block in a city as alive and magical as New York? Not a real writer, that's for sure."**

"I got inspired," Mikki said lightly. She grabbed Elizabeth by the arm, dragging her into the art studio. "Look," Mikki breathed. "I'm in a painting phase again."

Elizabeth truly didn't know what to say. Mikki was in a painting phase, all right—she'd produced swirling color canvases of such energetic brilliance they were enough to keep a person up for days. But there was more. Mikki hadn't just filled up the four canvases in the room, she'd filled the walls. A mural started beside the door and spread all around the room, stopping only to make way for the windows.

"I love New York," Mikki said. "See this here? That's Tompkins Square Park, all the people, the energy, those boys on the bicycles, see all the spinning blue and yellow? That's them. Here, this is the roof deck—I added in some stars. And that's Madison Avenue. It so abstract, but I think the feeling's there, yeah? Do you love it?"

"Mikki, it's gorgeous," Elizabeth said.

"I know," Mikki said. "I'm so inspired here. I know *you* know what I mean."

"Definitely," Elizabeth said automatically—it seemed like the only answer. Who would have writer's block in a city as alive and magical as New York? Not a real writer, that's for sure. "But," Elizabeth started, her old, more responsible self coming through, "don't you think you're going to get in trouble?"

"For what?" Mikki seemed honestly confused by the

question. "I know I'm the Photography intern, but there's no rule against painting. Art is art, and this is the kind of art I'm into right now. Tomorrow it could be something totally different. You follow?"

"No, I mean don't you think you'll get in trouble when Emma sees what you did to the room? I mean, you painted all over her *walls*."

Is Mikki truly that oblivious?

"Huh," Mikki said, picking at the green glob of paint in her hair. "Guess I'm not the full quid tonight—didn't even think she'd be upset." Then she shrugged. "Ah, no worries, I'll paint it over when I leave."

"I guess," Elizabeth said. She couldn't fathom what it would be like to be so free-spirited, so unafraid to do what she wanted, when she wanted.

"Glad you're the first of my mates to see this," Mikki said. "You're the creative genius of the bunch, and if you like it then I'm stoked."

"Oh, I do. But creative genius? Funny," Elizabeth said. She wanted to tell Mikki then and there how much trouble she was having.

I'm not as good as you think I am, she wanted to say. *And soon enough everyone will find out.*

"No joke," Mikki continued. "You're writing a novel. That's brilliant. I admire you so much, Lizzy."

Elizabeth swallowed her confession. Mikki was the coolest girl she had ever known. She was creative every second of the day. She even made sculptures out of her food while she was eating! No way would she understand.

"Thanks," Elizabeth said.

"I'm zonked," Mikki said. "I'll catch an hour and then onto that meeting with Ms. Bishop." She winked at Elizabeth. "I'd better come up with an idea to pitch, and fast!"

Me too, Elizabeth thought as she gazed around at the room-size painting. *I need an idea, too.*

chapter five

L et's hear all the pitches," Ms. Bishop announced at the Monday meeting. "Georgia, I already know what yours is, but I'd like an update. Let's start with you."

Everyone in the conference room turned to look at Georgia. At the table were all the interns, all the department heads, and even Delia, Ms. Bishop's assistant, there with her pen aloft to take notes.

Yet Georgia wasn't concerned—she'd come prepared. She'd spent countless hours that weekend on her article about Eve Bridges. Every word of that two-hundred word piece had been carefully sculpted into the three-paragraph opus she'd finished at the stroke of midnight Sunday night.

"It's done, actually," Georgia said. She pulled the typed page from her folder and passed it across the table to Ms. Bishop. The other girls eyed her in admiration. *No one thinks I'm serious about this. But I so am. Georgia Cooper, TV star. Georgia Cooper, star writer. Georgia Cooper—*

Ms. Bishop passed the page back to Georgia. "Read it," she said.

"What, out loud?" Georgia said. She could feel the blood rising to her cheeks. She bet her freckles looked like bright red polka-dots right about now.

"Ick. That's sweet enough to give me bulimia."

"Yes, aloud," Ms. Bishop said. "Think of it as a table read, Georgia."

"Okay," Georgia said. Before scenes are filmed on a TV or movie set, actors often do a first read of the script just sitting around a table. It was like a rehearsal, but really casual. Georgia had done it hundreds of times. But now? Here? In front of all these magazine people?

Georgia picked up her page. "Eve Bridges is not the typical soap star," she began reading. The story kept on like that—all happy-go-lucky like she and Eve had become BFF over iced tea, like she did not in fact hate Eve's guts and wish to throw her under the wheels of the first passing cab. Georgia finished with the last line: "Watching Eve is like looking onto paradise. She'll be making paradise of the big screen again soon."

Then she looked up, a wide smile on her face. In seconds, the smile was gone, because no one—not one single person—was smiling back.

"Ick," Demetria said. "That's sweet enough to give me bulimia."

"It wasn't that bad," Trey cut in, glaring at the Fashion editor.

"But it was . . . bad?" Georgia said.

"I don't feel like I got to know her," Mikki burst out.

"I mean Eve. Who *is* she?"

"She's an actress," Georgia said. *Obviously.*

"I get that," Mikki said. "But who is she as a person?"

"What do you think, Elizabeth?" Ms. Bishop asked.

Why is she asking Elizabeth? What, is she the be-all and end-all of opinions?

"I think it's . . ." Elizabeth hesitated. She met eyes with Georgia, and Georgia felt a glimmer of hope.

She'll have my back. We're both writers.

"I think it's trite, actually," Elizabeth said. "Both Mikki and Ms. Tish are right. We need to know who Eve Bridges is. We need to know why she's special enough to merit a piece in *Flirt*. Otherwise I think it's a waste of space, you know?"

Waste of space? Now Georgia wanted to throw Elizabeth under the wheels of a cab. *Do you want to know why Eve Bridges is the subject of my article? Because Ms. Bishop MADE me write about her!*

"I'm sorry," Elizabeth added. "I'm just being honest."

"All right," Ms. Bishop said, clapping her hands. She turned to the next intern. "Asha, your turn. Let's hear your pitch."

"Wait," Georgia cut in. "That's it? Are you publishing it or not?"

Ms. Bishop's eyes held steady on Georgia's for a moment. "I'll decide this afternoon what will be considered. Right now I want to hear *all* the pitches."

"Okay," Georgia said. And right now she wanted to crawl under the table and hide there for the rest of the meeting. She had just written trite, bulimia-inducing garbage.

Georgia was quiet as the other girls pitched their projects. Asha had an idea for a sidebar on a new kind of face mask for the "New Faces" issue. Ms. Bishop called it clever, but Georgia wasn't impressed. She also wasn't impressed by Nova's DIY designs or Sivya's idea about new technologies. Mikki's photography project-in-progress (if it could even be called photography; it used more paint than anything else) seemed totally random. Georgia suspected she'd just whipped it up in her cubicle. Georgia's roommate, Nailah, was so shy, no one could hear her when she started her pitch. "Speak up," Ms. Bishop called across the table, and Nailah jumped in her chair like she was at some kind of sporting event. Georgia didn't get Nailah—she had a pretty decent idea about new treatments for sports injuries, and she'd done a lot of research, but she had no confidence.

Confidence would not be lacking in Elizabeth. "And we're all excited to hear what you've come up with," Ms. Bishop said.

"I—" Elizabeth started. She met Georgia's eyes for

a moment and there was a shot of energy across the table. Georgia knew suddenly what was about to happen next. Somehow, she just knew.

She's going to get slammed, Georgia thought, her heart beating fast at the thought. This would make her day.

"It's an article . . ." Elizabeth said, hesitating.

She's nervous. She knows it's no good.

"Of course," Ms. Bishop said. "Go on, Elizabeth."

"It's really rough at the moment," Elizabeth said.

A shadow hovered on Ms. Bishop's face.

Georgia's heart was practically in her throat.

Then Ms. Bishop's assistant, Delia, cut in—she was waving her hand, headphones jammed into her ears. "Ms. Bishop, I'm sorry to interrupt, but it's Bob again."

"Again?" Ms. Bishop said, breaking her gaze from Elizabeth's imminent failure.

Oh, don't stop now!

"He says it's urgent," Delia said.

Ms. Bishop stood. "Elizabeth, come see me later. Everyone else, good work. I look forward to parsing through your ideas. Delia, transfer the call to my office."

And at that, Ms. Bishop was gone and the meeting was adjourned. The department heads left the conference room, leaving only the interns.

"That sucked," Nova said. "Let's hear your idea anyway, Lizzy. Pitch it to us."

"Yes, tell us," Asha said. "You've been so secretive about it all weekend."

"I sort of can't," Elizabeth said.

"You're going to tell Ms. Bishop anyway," Georgia said. She, too, wanted to hear the brilliant idea. That way, she could find some way to tear it apart.

"No, I mean, I can't tell you my idea because I don't have one. I was just going to come up with something on the spot. That Bob guy called at the exact right moment."

"You must be kidding!" Asha said, horrified.

"You got real lucky," Nova remarked.

"Seems to be happening a lot lately," Georgia grumbled.

"What's that supposed to mean?" Mikki said. "Lizzy would have come up with something, no doubt. She's really talented."

"So I've *heard*," Georgia said. She gathered her things. "I have a story to rewrite. I don't want it to be *trite* or anything." At that, she left the room.

☙   ☙   ☙   ☙

From: bishop@flirt.com
To: elizabeth_c@flirt.com, georgia_c@flirt.com, mikki_a@flirt.com, sivya_l@flirt.com, asha_p@flirt.com, nailah_j@flirt.com, nova_b@flirt.com
Cc: delia_z@flirt.com
Re: Short list for "New Faces" issue

Girls,

After our meeting this morning, I've determined
which interns should continue on with their pieces
for possible inclusion in the next issue: Mikki,
Nailah, Asha, and Elizabeth. I want your projects
Friday latest to allow time for my edits.
For the rest of you: There is always next issue.

—JB

ⓖ　　ⓖ　　ⓖ　　ⓖ

Georgia had forced her way into Ms. Bishop's
office. No appointment, no announcement, not even any
permission. Before Ms. Bishop could throw her out, she
started talking.

"Ms. Bishop, I just don't think it's fair. I wasn't even
pitching my own idea. That was an assignment *you* gave
me. I would've written something else if I had the chance
to! Everyone else got to come up with their own pitches,
so I should, too. I want another shot. I don't want to write
about the soap star; I wanted to write something *real*."

It had come out in a flood and then she stood there,
shaken.

*Did I really just have a fit in front of the editor-in-
chief?*

Oddly enough, Ms. Bishop didn't seem upset. She

didn't yell or point all icy-hot to the door. "I blame myself," she said.

"Uh, what?" Georgia asked.

"You need more direction, Georgia. You've been here a week without your own mentor, and I realize, you're right, it's not fair to you."

Speaking of unfair, talk to Elizabeth about doing her work like everyone else.

Ms. Bishop continued. "But I want you to know I am closing in on hiring a new Entertainment editor. I have a final interview with my top choice candidate later today."

"Okay," Georgia said. "So can I have another chance? With my own idea?"

"I'm listening . . ." Ms. Bishop said.

"I don't have an idea yet. Don't close me out, Ms. Bishop. I have name recognition. Having an article by me would be great for your magazine."

"Is that so?"

"Yeah," Georgia said, losing a bit of her own confidence.

What she didn't say was: *You know an article by me would sell more issues than anything by this nobody Elizabeth Whateverwood.*

"All right," Ms. Bishop said. "But not because of your fame, Georgia. Because you're willing to go the extra mile and I appreciate that. Just like I told the other girls, your deadline is Friday."

"Thank you, Ms. Bishop," Georgia said. She practically ran for the door.

"And Georgia, look through back issues of the magazine for inspiration, all right? Delia can give you the key to the Library."

"Yeah, okay, sure, no problem," Georgia said. Then she kept running. She had a work of genius to produce, and she had only a smattering of days to do it.

☉   ☉   ☉   ☉

Before Georgia even made it to the supposed *Flirt* Library, she discovered a message on her cell phone. And the message was one she'd been waiting on for months— *be honest*—years. It was her talent agency, saying they had news for her and she should call them back.

Whatever news it is, it's too little, too late, she thought.

After *Molly Mack*'s cancellation, she'd begged them for more work—on TV, movies, TV movies, anything. But nada, except for a few commercials here and there. Her only claim to fame in the years that followed was dating that jerk, Anton Stone. And dating a star didn't make you a star (especially when he dumped you after a few months).

But she had to call her agency back. News was news. After years of no news, she couldn't help but be . . . curious.

"This is Georgia Cooper, returning your call," she said when she reached the agent who had replaced her original agent, some guy named James Nakazawa.

"Georgia, how soon can you get here? I can fit you in at two."

"Mr. Nakazawa . . . James, I can't get to your office at two. I'm in New York."

"What are you doing in New York?"

"I'm a summer intern at *Flirt* magazine. Don't you read the gossip websites? Stalkerazzi's posted about this, like, twenty times."

"Oh, who reads Stalkerazzi? Only half of what they put up there is true. But seriously, you're in New York? A fashion intern, now that's a shocker."

"What's the news? Can't you tell me over the phone?"

"You have an audition. We know you've been frustrated about your dry spell"—talk about an understatement—"but people needed some time to get Molly Mack out of their minds. Enough time has passed. It's time to restart your career, Georgia."

> **"Only half of what they put up there is true. But seriously, you're in New York? A fashion intern, now that's a shocker."**

But.

But she'd decided to give up on acting. She'd even gone so far as to tell Ms. Bishop she was giving it up!

"I don't want to do another commercial, James. I told you, I'm an intern now. This summer is going to be really busy and I just don't have the time to—"

"It's a film," James interrupted. "Esteban Mirra's new film. He asked for you specifically."

Georgia went numb. Her hand almost lost hold of her cell phone. Esteban Mirra was an up-and-coming director known all over Europe and the United States. His first film went to Venice and Cannes. This was the opportunity of a lifetime. For someone who still wanted to be an actor, anyway.

"Georgia, are you there? Are you interested? Can you be here tomorrow?"

"Yes," Georgia said. "I mean yes, I want the audition, but I can't fly there tomorrow. Could you send my reel or something? I can't just leave—"

"Actually, I'm thinking we can arrange something in New York. Just keep your calendar free for the next few days. I'll be in touch."

Then the call cut out and she was still holding her phone. It took her a good few seconds to remember to flip it closed and put it down.

"Ohmigod ohmigod ohmigod," Georgia said to herself. How could she turn down this audition? And yet how would she be able to keep her calendar free while interning at *Flirt*?

Then she noticed a head peeking up over the wall of her cubicle. It was her neighbor, Sivya. "Hi," Sivya said. "You're not going to bail on us, are you?"

"You were eavesdropping, hmm?" Georgia said.

"I can't help it. I have bat hearing. So are you?"

"Let's not talk about this here, okay?"

"Want lunch?" Sivya seemed confused and excited and supportive all at once. "My treat."

"Sivya, you're not buying me lunch."

"If I don't, you won't tell me all the gossip, and I'm dying to hear. Please?"

Georgia didn't need too much convincing. She wanted someone to talk to. And here was Sivya, practically begging. It was like starting up a whole new entourage from scratch. She had to let *somebody* in.

They bought hot dogs on the street and sat in a nearby park. Georgia found herself opening up, saying how stung she'd felt after the meeting and how elated she felt about the audition. "Please don't tell anyone," she begged Sivya. "I mean, who knows how it'll go. Auditions are the worst. They could take one look at me and send me packing."

"I doubt that," Sivya said. "But Georgia, for real . . . what if you get it?"

Georgia couldn't keep the smile off her face. "That would be a miracle."

"I mean, how would you do a movie and work at *Flirt* at the same time?"

"Then fate would be really cruel," Georgia joked.

Sivya was being serious. She usually liked to make light of things, but not today.

"I dunno. I'd have to choose one or the other, I guess."

"You'd choose the movie. Right?"

Georgia shoved the rest of her hot dog in her mouth instead of answering. When she looked up, she saw the cameras. She groaned. "Beautiful," she said. "Now I'm going to be all over the Web with mustard on my face."

Sivya checked her own mouth for mustard. "Do you ever want to just freak out at them, like stick out your tongue and start screaming?" She had a glimmer in her eyes. "If I had cameras on me all the time, I'd want to do something crazy. Just to see what would happen."

Georgia shrugged. "It's just normal for me. There've always been cameras."

"That's weird."

"You know what would be weird? If, like, there were suddenly no cameras, and nobody was watching, and no one cared." Sivya listened, nodding. Georgia felt like she was saying too much.

"Is that why you dated Anton Stone? For the attention?"

"What?! No way."

Sivya shrugged. "He *is* cute." Then she shielded her face. "Oh no. That guy with the ugly shirt and the really huge camera is coming over here."

"*Ugh*, Joey Joey. He follows me everywhere. C'mon, let's run."

They trashed their hot dog wrappers and ran as fast as they could for the Hudson-Bennett building. Georgia felt the thrill of being chased, even if it was only by one old guy with a camera so heavy he couldn't run that fast. She felt the wind in her hair and the eyes of the crowd on her and the whole world at her fingertips.

She had an audition, for a movie. She had another shot.

ⓖ   ⓖ   ⓖ   ⓖ

Georgia didn't have much of a chance to get comfortable at her desk. Features and Entertainment were having some kind of closed-door meeting and they needed someone to go on a coffee run. There was a coffee machine in every kitchen, but no—these magazine people insisted on brand-name coffee concoctions instead.

Georgia couldn't blame them: She wouldn't drink the dark sludge that came out of those machines, either. But didn't they have some lowly assistant to take care of it? Some lackey to carry ice-cold and scorching-hot liquids in and out of the building like a waitress-in-training or a . . .

Then it dawned on her. *I guess that's the point of having interns,* she realized.

She was making her way through the lobby, somehow balancing two trays containing eight drinks total, when she saw him again: the most beautiful bike messenger in all of Manhattan. *What's-his-name. Oh, right, Tyler.*

He was coming out while she was going in. His curly black hair was in his eyes and he let it dangle there, adorable. He had his bike balanced over his shoulder, his pants with the one leg up, one leg down that she just loved. She peeked down to get a look at his one bare shin.

"Hi," she said as she tiptoed past. She was wearing white Stella McCartney pants and she so did not want a spill. "See you maybe tomorrow?"

He backed up, wheeling the bike beside her. "Hey, yourself. Looks like you could use some help with those." He held out his free arm for one of the drink trays.

Georgia wasn't one to be all coy when a guy was offering to carry her junk. "Sure," she said, letting him take the tray.

"So," he said, "guess what I did last night?"

"A wheelie over the Empire State Building?"

"No, that's not possible," he said, grinning. And that's when she noticed the dimple. There it was on his cheek, visible only when he smiled.

"Go on," she said. They were standing in the middle

of the Hudson-Bennett lobby. Everyone there could see them talking, just a bicycle and two trays of sweating iced coffee between them. She didn't care who saw.

"I looked you up online," he said. "Georgia Cooper. I read all about you."

"You did?" She kept her voice light.

Is this good or bad? Good, surely, because he made the effort. But bad because of what he found? WHAT could he have found?

"So you're a detective, huh?"

"Just on TV. And not anymore—if you looked me up, you know my show was canceled a long time ago. So what else did you find out?"

Let's stand here and talk about me for the rest of the day.

She allowed herself one little fantasy of riding on the front handlebars of Tyler's bike while he steered—zooming down Broadway with the lights and the sounds of the city all in a blur around them . . .

"So are you still seeing that Anton Stone guy or what?" Tyler asked.

Her fantasy broke into little jagged pieces all over the lobby floor. Just hearing the name Anton Stone was a buzz kill.

"I don't want to talk about that," she said in the sweetest voice she could muster. Why did people have to rub her face in the worst breakup of her life? Okay, her only breakup, but still, it sucked because *he* dumped *her* and everyone in the whole entire universe knew about it.

"You know what?" she continued. "I've got to get these coffees upstairs. The editors are drowsy and dehydrated—not a good combination." She reached for the tray.

"What did I say?" Tyler said. He wasn't about to give up that tray. "I was just asking . . ."

"Everybody's always asking," Georgia said. "And I guess I'm just tired of answering."

Tyler shrugged. "I'm still helping you bring the drinks upstairs. Even if you're not talking to me."

Georgia's little fantasy bubbled up again—the handlebars, the city lights, and don't forget the wind in her long, gorgeous red hair . . .

"Are we going up or what?" Tyler said. The dimple was showing again.

"Yes, let's."

They headed for the elevator bank and stepped onto one just before the doors closed. A woman was already in the elevator, black power suit, briefcase, and deadly heels that rivaled the height of Ms. Bishop's. She had sleek highlighted hair cut to the nape of her neck. Her round Harry Potter–style glasses hinted at a sense of whimsy.

She took one look at Georgia and said, "I know you."

Georgia glanced at Tyler. He had a smug look of amusement on his face.

"Yeah, I'm Georgia Cooper," Georgia said, "and I don't mind doing an autograph. Do you have a pen?" She felt so silly saying all of that in front of Tyler—he was so far from starstruck around her, it was almost endearing—but it was her usual spiel. And why not show him that she was generous and friendly with her fans?

The elevator had reached *Flirt*'s floor, and the woman in the power suit got off, too. "Oh, I don't need an autograph, Georgia. Don't you remember me? Jane Wolander, I did that story on you in *LA Week*, the 'Where Is She Now?' feature."

Georgia took a deep look in those eyes—those owl-like glasses in the way—and remembered. People did those kinds of stories on her a lot, but this particular one, for one of her hometown magazines, was not a favorite. The 'where is she now?' question was answered with 'nowhere' and 'doing nothing'—Jane Wolander had not been impressed by Georgia's lack of career.

"Silly me, how could I forget," Georgia said. "You called me a has-been and said I was too afraid to start over, but you were wrong, because look where I am now." Georgia held out the tray and it sort of dribbled on the knee of her white capris.

"*Flirt* is featuring a story on you? Georgia, that's just great."

"Not exactly," Georgia said. "I'm not in the magazine, I'm writing for it now."

"That's incredible!" Jane said. "Do you remember our interview? How you said you had an interest in writing? You wanted to write a memoir about your childhood in the TV limelight, as I recall. How's that coming?"

"It's not. Not yet. I mean, yes, I am writing for the magazine. But as a summer intern. I'm the Entertainment intern here."

Jane's smile didn't waver. "Georgia, that's just wonderful. Congratulations."

"Thanks," Georgia said, feeling shy all of a sudden. She knew it was a big leap between Hollywood star and *Flirt* intern, but it was a leap she'd *wanted* to take. She was proud of taking it. It was the first chance she'd had to try to be a writer.

Jane seemed impressed. Georgia glanced again at Tyler. He seemed impressed, too. And he was still holding all that coffee.

"Even better," Jane said, leaning in toward Georgia. "I am right now on my way to my final interview with Jo Bishop. I recently moved to New York, and she's considering me for the Entertainment editor position."

"That means . . ." Georgia started.

Jane raised an eyebrow.

". . . that you'd be my boss. And I'd be getting *you* coffee."

"Interesting," Jane said. She headed for the reception desk to sign in.

Tyler and Georgia were left standing there with their coffee trays.

"It took me so long to get the coffee, their meeting's probably over by now," Georgia said, but she made no move for the door.

"Tell them there was a really long line," he said.

"I'll do that."

"You should go."

"Yeah, totally." She waited a beat, then took the second tray from him and headed for the entrance to the *Flirt* offices. Coffee had leaked on her clothes and she didn't care.

"Hey," he called out, running his bike over the carpet while he talked.

She turned.

"So, you never did answer my question. Are you still seeing that guy or what?"

"No," she said. "I am most definitely not."

"Good," he said.

ⓖ   ⓖ   ⓖ   ⓖ

Back in the office, Georgia made a disturbing discovery. One of the iced coffees on the trays she'd broken her back carrying to the office was not for the editors in their closed-door meeting—it was for Elizabeth Cheekwood.

She's an intern! She can get her own coffee!

"You don't mind bringing it to her, do you?" Caitlain said in the conference room. She was distracted. She and the other staff members had pages spread out over the table and were trying to narrow down a presentation for Ms. Bishop.

"Where's Elizabeth, then?" Georgia asked.

"Oh, she was here," Caitlain said, "but the meeting was running long and we let her take off to work on her article."

Elizabeth was invited to the closed-door meeting and not me? What am I, chopped liver?

"Sure, I'll bring Elizabeth her coffee," she said, leaving the room.

And then I'll dump it all over her pretty blond head.

She marched over to Elizabeth's cubicle. Empty. She peeked around the area. No Elizabeth. She went to Ms. Bishop's office—door closed.

"You haven't seen Elizabeth, have you?" Georgia asked Delia, behind her usual spot at the desk.

"Yes, she has the key," Delia said distractedly.

"The key to what?"

"The Library. Ms. Bishop said she wanted you in there doing research for your project, but Elizabeth took it first, so you'll have to share."

Georgia had it in mind to pour out the coffee in the

sink, but she had a little itch of curiosity. Ms. Bishop had told Elizabeth to go to the Library, too? That meant they were both in need of some direction.

Maybe Lizzy's not as hot as she thinks she is.

The Library was stowed in the far back of one of *Flirt*'s less glamorous hallways. Georgia hadn't even known it was there. She pushed the door in to find Elizabeth sitting on the floor, a sea of magazines all around her. Georgia recognized the titles: *Flirt*'s competition, *Flirt*'s little sisters, *Flirt*'s crazy half-cousins from the mountains. Just like the mythic Closet for clothes—Georgia had only heard it existed; she still hadn't seen it—the Library contained any known fashion publication past, present, or future, some so old their yellowed pages were cast in specially cut coats of plastic.

"Boo," Georgia said.

Elizabeth jumped. She covered a few of the magazines, like she didn't want Georgia to steal her ideas.

"So," Georgia said, careful not to step on a *Vogue*, "doing research for your killer story? That must mean you have an idea. What is it?"

Elizabeth deflected the question. "Um, is that coffee mine?"

"Yeah, it's yours," Georgia said. "Did Ms. Bishop send you here?"

"What? No. Why would she?"

Because she thinks you need help, hmm?

But no. Elizabeth was here by her own choice. She wasn't in trouble.

Georgia placed the iced coffee on the floor far enough away so that Elizabeth would have to reach for it—the ice had melted so it looked like dirty puddle water. She pointed at the brown stain on her white Stella McCartney knee. "You owe me," she said.

Elizabeth noted the stain. "Omigod, it spilled."

Georgia nodded. "I do not do deliveries for other interns. Next time there's a coffee run, it's on you. Got it?"

"Yeah, okay," Elizabeth said. Then she waited, like she couldn't page through the magazines with Georgia in the room.

I don't want to hang with her anyway, Georgia thought. She heaved a sigh and headed for the door. She'd just come back later, do her work alone.

"Thanks, Georgia," Elizabeth called out before the door closed.

I hope you get locked in here and never come out, Georgia thought. Then she had second thoughts. She'd go one better . . . *I hope you write the worst story in the whole universe and Ms. Bishop decides not to publish it. And then she publishes mine instead.*

Smiling as if for a camera, Georgia returned to her desk.

stalkerazzi.com

Currently stalking . . . Georgia Cooper . . . spotted at the soon-to-be-lukewarm club BED for a mere hour before she ran off to make her "curfew." Anton Stone, the dumb stiff who dumped her, was nowhere to be found. In other Georgia news, we hear tell that a certain Cannes favorite has asked for Georgia specifically for his new movie. But this doesn't mean a guaranteed marquee—Georgia has to audition for the role like anyone else. When asked how insulted she is, she said, and we quote, "How did you find that out? Are you stalking me?" Yes, Georgia darling, we are. Now do us proud and break a leg or a toe or something. We'd pay the ten+ bucks to see your face on the big screen!

Elizabeth checked Stalkerazzi often. She was curious about Georgia. For instance, who knew that when Georgia told the girls she needed to "get some air," she wasn't on the roof, as everyone assumed, but making an appearance at a club?

Georgia made it seem as if she didn't like Elizabeth, but Elizabeth just wouldn't accept that. She couldn't stand the thought of someone disliking her.

Georgia's not being mean to me, Elizabeth told herself whenever Georgia made a snide comment. *She's just moody. Or weird. Or not used to making friends. Or . . . it has to be SOMETHING.*

And the more excuses she made for Georgia, the more curious she got.

The girls usually took the subway to work together every morning. Georgia would make a fuss about how she'd rather take a cab, but more often than not she'd go with them.

This morning, on the way to the subway, Elizabeth walked beside Georgia, asking questions. At first, Georgia was only too happy to talk about herself.

"I'm an only child," Georgia was saying. "My mom moved to Hollywood when I was four so we could pursue my career. She was a waitress at Winky's. She sacrificed everything so I could get where I am; that's why I bought her the house. Hey, haven't you heard all this already? I talk about it all the time in interviews."

"No, no, go on," Elizabeth said. The other girls had gone ahead, so it was just the two of them. "So what was it like being on such a popular TV show?"

"Seriously, why all the questions all of a sudden?"

"I'm just, I don't know . . . curious." Yes, she was

curious, selfishly curious. Georgia's exciting life was giving her some ideas.

They'd reached the Prince Street subway stop. "I've got a question for you," Georgia said as they headed down the stairs to catch the train. "What's your story about? Not about me, right?"

Would it be so wrong to say that I'm thinking about it? Elizabeth thought.

Georgia stopped on the stairs. "Please tell me you're not writing about me."

Elizabeth was unable to meet Georgia's piercing green eyes. "I'm just asking questions, that's all," she said lamely as they pushed through the turnstiles.

Their other roommates were already on the platform. Sivya, Mikki, and Asha were talking with their heads close together, giggling quietly. Nova was standing with her toes at the edge of the platform, looking bored. Nailah was off by herself on the bench—she was so shy, it was easy to forget she was there. Each of those girls had a story. And then there was Georgia, studiously oblivious of the people stealing glances at her.

The train barreled into the station. The wind picked up Georgia's long red hair, flinging it about her shoulders. Elizabeth couldn't help staring, just like everyone else.

I think I might change my whole entire novel, she thought. It was a scary thought, but she couldn't help but be pulled along with it.

The train screeched to a stop. Georgia started yelling to Elizabeth over the noise. "Seriously, Lizzy, if you're writing your article about me, you have to tell me. You can't just take things I say off the record and put them in your story. That's not how it works. Believe me, I've been interviewed tons of times and I know."

"I never said I was writing my article about you!" Elizabeth said, but her words were drowned out by the train. It stopped and the doors opened.

But it was a fabulous idea. Not for the article—she'd had a little inspiration on that yesterday when she was peeking through magazines in the Library. She'd even borrowed a few magazines (i.e., shoved them in her bag) for ideas—no one needed to know.

It was her book that needed some life breathed into it. And her agent wasn't happy with the Great Big Nothing she was getting.

Writing about Georgia is the best idea I've had all week, Elizabeth thought. She floated onto the train, grabbed a silver pole, and held on all the way to Times Square.

    ⓖ   ⓖ   ⓖ   ⓖ

It was Thursday after work—one night to deadline—

"Seriously, Lizzy, if you're writing your article about me, you have to tell me."

and Elizabeth had everything she needed to write her *Flirt* article: her favorite fountain pen that had once belonged to her granddad, her fuzzy yellow writing slippers, a glass of honey-sweetened iced tea, peace and quiet, and—

"Lizzy!" The shrieking of her name continued until she left the desk in her bedroom and peeked down the stairs.

Mikki was in one of her high-energy moods. "We *must* go to this Vietnamese place near Nova's apartment and we must get noodles and we must do it now. Get changed. You're coming with."

Nova was on the couch, stretching lazily. "I just said I was craving Saigon Grill. I didn't say we had to go right now."

"Now," Mikki insisted. "Who's coming? Lizzy, I knew you'd be in. Asha, no point asking, she has that homework. What about Nailah?" She turned to the far corner of the loft, where Nailah could be seen doing yoga with her headphones on. Elizabeth wondered what was going on with Nailah. Was she homesick?

"Forget Nailah," Nova said. "She never wants to go anywhere. Besides, Saigon Grill can be sorta greasy and it's all the way uptown. Where's Sivya?"

"I don't know. I think up on the roof—with Georgia?" Elizabeth put in.

"Oh god, let's bounce before Georgia invites herself," Nova said, donning her largest sunglasses. "I'm so not in the mood to get my picture taken."

Elizabeth had her laptop open on her desk upstairs. She had hundreds of words to write in a single night and maybe she should have been up there, working.

But a girl's got to eat, right?

6   6   6   6

By the time Elizabeth returned to the loft, it was about eight o'clock. Nothing to worry about—she was amped up on the ultra-sweet Vietnamese iced coffees that Nova insisted on ordering. She could write all night, for hours, for days . . .

Now that's an idea. What I need are a few days. If only I had the weekend . . .

Then it dawned on her. She *could* have the weekend. It was as simple as telling Ms. Bishop that she'd had a computer crash and lost her work. She'd say that she'd retype it over the weekend. She'd say she'd make it better than it was before.

She closed her laptop and went downstairs to the living room. A bunch of the girls were there, too, watching TV. And it wasn't just any TV show—it was *Flirt It!*, the reality show sponsored by the very magazine she was interning for. The show was just one of many projects Ms. Bishop had her hands in at any given moment. The premise of the show was to search for upcoming models; the winner would be on the cover of *Flirt*.

"I hope Adonia wins," Sivya said. "I love her nose. She's definitely my favorite."

"You want someone to win because of a *nose*?" Nova said. "Watch Svetlana walk the runway. No one can beat her."

"I like Brittany," Asha called from the kitchen. She had mounds of chem homework to do, and she'd taken all her science equipment from her bedroom to set up a makeshift lab on the kitchen counter. She was mixing something with goggles on as she watched the show.

"You can't like Brittany. She was cut the second week!" Mikki called.

"I cannot believe you guys like this show," Georgia said, sniffing. "Reality TV is death to good, scripted shows. You have no idea how hard it is on us actors."

Elizabeth was effectively sucked in. She found a spot on the couch beside Mikki.

During a commercial, Asha sprang out of the kitchen with a bowl of something sticky.

"What is that? Wax?" Nova said, peering into the bowl.

"It's my latest chemistry experiment," Asha announced.

> ❝ *Reality TV is death to good, scripted shows. You have no idea how hard it is on us actors.* ❞

"Is it food?" Georgia asked.

"At least you didn't mix that gunk in our room," Nova said. "It's a toxic waste dump in there."

Asha rolled her eyes. "Who wants to try it, then?" She held out the bowl.

"You didn't answer me," Georgia said. "Is it edible or not?"

"You don't eat it! It's lip stain. For your lips," Asha said. She turned to Nailah. "Nailah, want to go first?"

Nailah looked up, startled. "You want me to . . . put that on my mouth?"

"It won't hurt," Asha said.

"You try it then," Georgia said.

Asha put some on her lips. At first her lips just looked shiny, and the same color, but soon they turned pink, then pinker, until they were a bright shade of rose.

"Pretty," Sivya said. "I'll try some."

"It's supposed to turn different colors, depending on what mood you're in," Asha explained. "Mostly pinks, I think."

On Sivya, the stain turned a pale salmon pink. "Nice," Nova said. She reached out and tried some, getting more of a fuchsia. Nailah got pale pink, too, and Mikki got a bright, brilliant color, fitting to her hyper mood.

Elizabeth put some on and then glanced in Asha's compact mirror. "I love it," she breathed. Her color was a cool pink that suited her.

"Fine," Georgia huffed. She reached out a finger and smoothed some on her lips. Then she smoothed on some more. "Tastes like raspberries," she said.

"Yeah, I used some fruit flavoring to, um, oh," Asha said. Her eyes went wide.

On Georgia's lips, the stain was very dark, and it was getting darker by the second. Finally it turned a deep, deep purple—like a bruise.

"That's strange," Asha said. She grabbed a paper towel and tried to wipe it off, but the color stayed.

"What?" Georgia said. She looked into the compact mirror and shrieked.

"It'll come off," Asha assured her. "Just go wash with soap and water."

Georgia stomped upstairs to the bathroom. The other girls returned to the TV show—aspiring models were practicing for the runway by balancing books on their heads—and it wasn't until the next commercial that Georgia emerged from the bathroom.

Asha took one look at her and said, "Oh no."

"What did you do to me?" Georgia said. Her eyes were blazing.

"The pigment must have stained your lips. Maybe try cold cream?" Asha said.

Nova was trying to stifle her laughter with her hand.

"You think this is funny, Nova?" Georgia said.

"No, it's just your face, Georgia. I actually like the color. I'd wear it."

"Can it," Georgia said. Then her eyes settled on Elizabeth and her bruise-colored mouth turned into a small smile. "Hey," she said, "don't you have that article to finish?"

"Yeah, I thought you said not to interrupt you for the rest of the night. Not even to go clubbing," Mikki said, nudging her.

True. I did say that, Elizabeth thought. *But now, with this "computer crash," I can watch TV all night.*

"It's okay," she said idly. "I lost the article, anyway. I'll just ask Ms. Bishop for an extension. Omigod, look: That one model is sabotaging that other one's shoes!"

"Wait, what? You lost your article?" Asha said. "How?"

Elizabeth shrugged. "My computer crashed and I lost it. I'll explain it to Ms. Bishop tomorrow."

"You seem awfully calm about the whole thing," Georgia observed, her eyes sharper and more intense than usual. She looked practically sinister with the dark mouth.

Does she know?

But before Elizabeth could get too nervous about Georgia knowing or not knowing, Sivya had leaped off the couch.

"Don't worry, Lizzy, I can fix any computer," Sivya

said. "You guys haven't seen yet what a whiz I am, for real. I'll retrieve your crash records—there's probably a saved copy of your document on your hard disk, you just don't know where to find it."

Elizabeth sat up straight, getting alarmed. "Sivya, watch the show, really. It's not fixable, you don't have to . . ." She stopped with the protests because Sivya had already run upstairs to the bedroom where Elizabeth had left her laptop.

Georgia didn't say a word. Elizabeth tried to smile, but Georgia didn't return it.

"I'd better go help Sivya," Elizabeth said. She climbed the spiral stairs slowly and entered her bedroom. Sivya was at the laptop, looking perplexed.

"Is it broken?" Elizabeth asked innocently.

"Um, no," Sivya said. "There's nothing wrong with it." She pointed at a black window with white type. "You haven't had a crash in over a week. It would be on this list. Are you sure you lost your file on this computer?"

Elizabeth shrugged.

"You were using this computer when it happened, right?" Sivya asked. She was speaking very slowly, as if to a child.

"Yeah," Elizabeth said.

"Did you delete it by accident?"

"Not exactly." Elizabeth approached the desk, standing close beside Sivya in the hopes that no one in the hallway could hear. "Sivya, can you keep a secret?"

Sivya hesitated, like she thought it was something really awful. "Sure, I guess."

"Please don't tell anyone, not even Georgia."

"I won't." Sivya looked uncomfortable.

"You don't have to do that," Elizabeth said, pointing to the laptop. "You can leave it alone."

Sivya typed EXIT and closed the window. "Because nothing went wrong with the computer," she said quietly.

Elizabeth nodded.

Sivya shook her head. "Lizzy, you're confusing me. What's going on?"

"I haven't written the article yet. That's the truth."

"But Ms. Bishop said she wanted it tomorrow. I heard her say Friday."

"Yeah, that's what she said," Elizabeth said. She looked meaningfully into Sivya's eyes. "Please don't tell, okay?"

"You want me to lie to Ms. Bishop?!" Sivya almost shrieked. Then she covered her mouth. "Lizzy, I can't do that, I just can't."

"No, of course not!" Elizabeth said. "I'd never ask you to lie." She looked away.

"Why don't you just *write* it?" Sivya said. She made it sound so easy.

"What, just sit in here and write it tonight?"

Sivya shrugged. "If I were you," she said slowly

and carefully, "I would try to do the project first before I lied about it."

There was a moment of silence. Elizabeth hung her head.

Sivya got one of her silly grins. "If anyone can write a genius article in one night, it's you, the literary genius." She poked Elizabeth in the side. "Know what I'm sayin'?"

Elizabeth shook her head, but she was a little ticklish, so she couldn't help but smile some. "I'm not a literary genius."

"Oh no? Who else wrote a novel at age sixteen, hmm? Best I've done is write a Perl script that automatically filters my e-mail and updates my address book. I am *such* a genius." She swept her messy ponytail over her shoulder.

Elizabeth giggled. "I haven't written the whole novel!" she said, but her mood had improved considerably. "Besides, I sent in some new pages to my agent and she hasn't e-mailed in days, so who knows. Maybe she doesn't want to be my agent anymore."

"That would never happen," Sivya said. "Anyway, I'm gonna go downstairs. You write. I'll tell you later which model gets booted tonight."

Then Elizabeth was left alone with only her laptop and her thoughts.

She had an article to write.

⊙　　⊙　　⊙　　⊙

Or sort of write. That was the problem—nothing was coming. She took a peek in some of the magazines she'd kept from *Flirt*'s Library. They were these tiny little magazines, with nowhere near the amount of readers as the big glossy she was interning for. Probably only a handful of people read these stories. Which gave her another idea.

Even if "Little Tiny Fashion Pub" had a story on XYZ, that didn't mean Ms. Bishop's writers had ever covered the topic of XYZ. It would be new to *Flirt*, technically.

Besides, Ms. Bishop couldn't read all the magazines in the Library. That would be physically impossible. Her eyes would burn out. She'd never have time to sleep.

It started off innocently enough. Elizabeth used an article about a young writer traveling to Mexico as a jumping-off point for her own story. She wrote a sentence, then another. Her roommates came in and out. At some point, Elizabeth took her laptop to one of the couches downstairs. The other girls talked around her, but she was in the zone, the words of her article forming in little bursts inside her head. Soon it would all come out, and she'd be done and donning her pajamas for bed.

The doorman called up to say someone had left a package for Georgia. The other girls teased her about it—flowers from her ex, Anton Stone?—but it was only a plain brown envelope, nothing that needed watering. Still, Georgia made a big scene about it as if she'd been delivered a loaner from Tiffany's.

"I'm going up to my chair on the roof," Georgia announced, hugging the package to her chest. "I need some air." Her lips were still as dark as a plum. She flounced up the stairs to the roof, and the girls laughed behind her back about Georgia's "chair"—the lawn recliner and umbrella she'd set up with the sheet. She hadn't let anyone else use it since she'd first arranged it.

Elizabeth heard this going on, but she wasn't all there. Soon the other girls scattered, and she was left alone in the living room.

I'm exhausted, she thought. She looked longingly up the stairs.

When she glanced back at her screen to read over what she'd written, there wasn't much there at all. *That's it? A few paragraphs?*

And did I mention how tired I am?

The next thing she did, she did without really thinking about it. She typed a sentence—the same exact sentence from the Mexico article. It was so easy; the thing was already written!

I'll edit it later, she thought wearily. *Just let me get the whole story down. Then I'll go back, change the words, rewrite it so it's my own.*

That was the plan. She had the best of intentions. There was no way she was showing up to work the next morning with nothing—no matter what.

chapter seven

Sivya was the only one who knew for sure about Georgia's audition. If any of the other roommates had read the rumor on Stalkerazzi, no one was telling. (And Georgia could always deny, deny, deny. That's acting, folks.) Georgia needed Sivya to keep it a secret, because she called in sick to work Friday morning so she could go. Before Sivya headed out with the rest of the girls for the subway, Georgia called her into her bedroom. She was in bed, cool washcloth over her forehead for effect.

"Do you need more water?" Sivya asked, genuinely concerned.

"No, I'm set," Georgia said. She peeked out from beneath the washcloth. "Sivya, we're getting to be friends, right?"

"Yeah!" Sivya said. "I hope. You sure you don't need more water?"

"So you didn't tell anyone about the Mirra audition, right? Because it's in two hours and I just told Delia to tell Ms. Bishop I have a migraine."

Sivya had a strained look on her face. "So I have to act like I don't know anything. Yeah okay, sure, no problem."

"It's just a little white lie."

"Yeah, I know. I have to go." Sivya pulled away. Then she turned back. She winked outrageously and said, "I predict that you will blow them away, Georgia." But as she was leaving, she mumbled, "I just hope you'll still be my friend when you do."

"Of course I will!" Georgia yelled. She was about to get out of bed when Emma came in. Quickly, Georgia flopped the washcloth back over her eyes and groaned dramatically. *"Uuuuuuuuuuuuuh,"* she said: the sound of indeterminate pain, probably migraine-related.

"Are you sure you'll be all right alone?" Emma asked. "I hate to leave you, but I just started teaching this course—"

"Please don't worry about me, really," Georgia cut in. She felt a pang of guilt for lying to her housemother, a really cool woman as far as housemothers go. "I'm feeling a little better," Georgia said, mustering up her thespian skills to look Emma directly in the eyes. "My migraine's almost gone. I think I'll just go in to work late."

"Okay, then," Emma said. "You have my cell number. And if you don't feel better, please stay home. My photo course lets out at two."

Georgia nodded. She kept her movements slow, figuring that's what people who actually had crippling migraines did. They probably talked slowly, too. (She really should have studied up on the role first.) "Bye, Emma," Georgia drawled.

"Feel better, Georgia," Emma said. Then she went downstairs.

Georgia counted to one hundred. She had to be patient. She had to make sure Emma hadn't forgotten anything and come back. By one hundred, she tiptoed out of her room. Then she slipped down the stairs. She peeked out the window and saw Emma hailing a cab and knew she was safe.

In seconds, she was leaping back up the spiral staircase toward her room. She had her audition outfit all picked out: black on black, with black shoes. It was inspired by Sivya, maybe, who only accessorized her black wardrobe with gray. More than that, Georgia was convinced that the all-black ensemble gave her the edge the casting directors would be seeking for this particular script. A copy of it had been messengered to her the night before. It was a daring role, the role of Nadia, and Georgia was shocked, and flattered, that Esteban Mirra was actually considering her to play it.

What part of Nadia does he see in me? Georgia thought as she wound her long red hair into a series of knots on her head. *The part where she's completely and totally selfish? Where she backstabs all her friends?*

I'm nothing like that. He must think I'm an incredible actress.

The thought made her feel incredibly flattered. And incredibly nervous.

She reached for some lipstick, then stopped. Her lips still had that dark tint from Asha's disastrous lip-stain experiment. And you know what? Her lips looked perfect for the character. She wasn't Molly Mack anymore; she was Nadia.

She tried saying one of the lines from the script into the mirror: "You don't hate me. You can't hate me. You never could."

Huzzah.

She barely recognized herself—she was that good.

⊙　　⊙　　⊙　　⊙

There was a moment during the audition when Georgia thought she was doing okay. It was maybe five seconds in. Then she lost it. It sure wasn't helping that she couldn't read the casting directors' faces, and that Esteban Mirra wasn't even in the room—they were videotaping the audition to send to him in Spain.

"You . . . don't . . . hate me," Georgia recited, the lines not having the same ferocity she remembered in the bathroom. "You can't hate me? You, um, never could?"

"Try it again," one of the casting directors called out. She had a face of stone. "With more feeling."

Georgia closed her eyes. She searched herself for some usable emotion. She wanted this. She also wanted to make it at *Flirt* and have everyone think she was great and have Ms. Bishop herself admit she was a super-talented writer and give her a chance at showing the whole entire world. Was that so much to ask? All that stood between her and that was a girl named Elizabeth Cheekwood.

Elizabeth Cheekwood. Good. She could use that.

She opened her eyes. Then she delivered her lines with energy. With passion. With a hard edge that surprised even herself. It was a miracle.

Georgia floated out of the audition. She'd rocked it. She hoped.

Out on the sidewalk, a flash went off in her face. Georgia's initial reaction was to give her usual smile and pose as always. Then it hit her: These photographs couldn't be published! She was supposed to be home sick with a migraine!

She ducked her head.

The flashing stopped. The photographer lowered his camera—Joey Joey, a familiar face. Today he wore a purple shirt with orange shorts and rubber flip-flops. It was a wonder no one turned around and photographed him right back.

"What's up, Georgia Cooper?" Joey Joey said. "No mood for the spotlight?"

"Joey Joey, can I be candid?" Georgia said. She felt like she knew Joey Joey; he'd been photographing her for years. He was almost—in some weird alter-reality where paparazzi weren't considered parasites—like family.

"Of course," Joey Joey said. "And can Joey Joey be candid with you, Georgia? This outfit today, that makeup . . . not working so much."

"It's temporary. Listen, Joey Joey, I don't mind your photos, you know that. That day with the mustard on my face, did I get mad? No. But you can't publish these photos today. I'm asking."

"You're denying your fans the chance to see this getup?"

"Yes." She leaned in—he smelled like patchouli and she tried not to sneeze. "I am not. Supposed. To. Be. Here," she whispered, enunciating each word. "Get it?"

As in, please do not sell my pictures so Ms. Bishop and Emma see them and know I lied about the sick day, okay?

"Say no more," he said. "Anton Stone is in there. I knew it."

"No!" Georgia shrieked.

"Okay, Georgia Cooper, okay. In exchange, how about you tell Joey Joey where you're *supposed* to be later." He winked.

"Work," she said, "till five thirty. Then home."

"Gotcha," Joey Joey said. Then, in an act of good faith, he put the lens cap on his camera.

◎ ◎ ◎ ◎

Ms. Bishop didn't blink an eye at the mention of a

migraine. "I've left a stack of work on your desk," was all she said when Georgia arrived halfway through the day.

So Georgia found herself at the photocopier, making copy after copy of Ms. Bishop's plans for the "New Faces" issue. In order to plan out the issue, she needed to "see it," Ms. Bishop had explained. These copies would be pinned up on the wall so she could see the "shape" of the issue and decide for sure what goes and what stays.

What a waste of time, Georgia thought. *Can't she look at a list or something?*

As Georgia was waiting for the copier to finish, Asha entered the copy room, an intense look of concern on her face. "Georgia, are you okay? Did my lip stain make you sick? Were you throwing up, or just the headache, or both? I hope it wasn't both."

"I'm fine, Asha, really," Georgia said. She found Asha somewhat amusing—so serious all the time, such a hard worker. Yet instead of doing her chemistry research, she had spent all of last night mixing makeup in the kitchen.

Asha reached out and felt Georgia's forehead. "You don't have a fever."

"Asha!" Georgia said. She wasn't used to strange girls touching her face.

"Georgia, I feel terrible. My parents want me to be a doctor, and look—I made you sick. If this isn't a reason to—"

"Stop, please!" Georgia closed the door to the copy room. "I didn't have a migraine, okay? I lied. I had an audition for a movie."

Asha's eyes widened. "You lied to Ms. Bishop!"

"Shh!" Georgia said.

A small smile played on Asha's lips. "So I didn't make you sick, then."

Georgia shook her head. "And, if you notice, your lip stain hasn't exactly washed off." She posed, puffing out her lips. "I kinda like it."

"Thanks," Asha said. "So, what are you copying? Oh, look, that's Lizzy's article!" She leaned in and started reading. "She's such a good writer."

"Is that so," Georgia said. Then she leaned in, too, so she could read for herself. The story was about traveling out of the country for the first time. "I thought Elizabeth had never left the East Coast," Georgia said.

Asha shrugged. "It says here she's been to Mexico. Anyway, I'm glad I didn't get you sick, Georgia. Relieved, in fact."

Georgia fake-swooned, leaning against the copier. "I got dizzy for a second."

"Don't joke," Asha said, seeming only about 75 percent serious. Then she left Georgia alone with her copies. And Elizabeth's article.

Georgia continued reading. And she really wished she hadn't. The story had a strong voice. It had rhythm. It was active, and exciting, and strong—all things she knew she needed in her own writing. It was not trite.

ⓖ   ⓖ   ⓖ   ⓖ

"Georgia, could you move over? Someone needs to see your computer." This was Shawn, the Photography assistant, hovering behind her with a tall, gorgeous girl who looked like a fashion model. That's because she was a fashion model. She was Alexa Veron—Georgia recognized her face—a former magazine intern herself.

"You want to see that weird girl's cartoons on my computer again, don't you?" Georgia grumbled. But she eyed Alexa as she moved aside, noting the girl's Bjorn V skinny jeans and bejeweled shirt.

"*Ay carambe!* That is hilarious!" Alexa shrieked. There were the dancing Kiyoko characters that Georgia was unfortunate enough to still have as a screen saver.

"I told you," Shawn said.

Alexa appeared to notice Georgia for the first time. "I know you," she said. "You are on TV." She stated it like a fact, not impressed or unimpressed.

"She *was* on TV," Shawn said. "A long time ago. Anyway, so Kiyoko made Georgia guess her login password for, like, three hours on her first day. It was so funny—"

"More like five minutes," Georgia said.

"Kiyoko can be"—Alexa searched for the word—"self-centered?"

"Arrogant," Shawn said.

"Difficult," Alexa said. "But we do love her for it."

Georgia stared back at them blankly. *And I care because . . . ?*

Sivya popped her head over the cubicle wall and waved to Alexa and Shawn. Mikki poked her head around, too. "I loved your photos, Alexa. The shots of the girl on the horse? Just brilliant. I'm Mikki, the new Photo intern, and this is Sivya, Electronic Content, and, ace, where did you get your necklace?"

Alexa laughed. "My hometown, Buenos Aires. Good to meet you, Mikki and Sivya and Georgia. What projects are you working on now?" She turned first to Georgia.

"Well, I *would* be writing an article," Georgia said. "If my pitch got accepted."

"Sorry," Sivya said.

"There's always next time," Mikki added.

"Bishop did not like your idea, then?" Alexa asked. "Then come up with another. I had to do that, more than a few times."

Georgia shrugged. "Too late. The deadline was today."

"She's right," Shawn said.

Alexa raised her eyebrows. "What is a deadline,

anyway? It is a line in the sand. It is an arbitrary date people tell you so you do what they want when they want it, *si?*"

"Exactly!" Mikki said.

Shawn chuckled uncomfortably. "I don't know about that . . ."

"What did Ms. Bishop say when she didn't want your idea? Did she say it was *muy* terrible and *muy* disgusting and you should go back to Catholic school rather than waste your time here?"

Georgia was having a hard time following. "I don't go to Catholic school."

"Doesn't matter, *muchacha*. My point is, did she say that she hates your writing?"

"No," Georgia said. "She just didn't say she liked it."

"Bueno!" Alexa shrieked.

"Um, huh?" Georgia said.

"I know how tough Top Diva can be, Shawn can attest"—he nodded vigorously—"but you have to know how to *interpret* her. It is like speaking another language."

"So . . ." Georgia prompted. All she figured Ms. Bishop was saying by not choosing her story for the magazine was: *It sucks, and so do you.* There it was, no translation necessary.

"Silence is *muy bueno*," Alexa said. "Silence is not no. No is no. You know what I think? I think you should write a new article this weekend. She says the deadline is today, but if Ms. Bishop wants something in, it goes in. Always."

Georgia shook her head. "I don't know," she said. But it's not like she wanted to go out without a fight.

"Georgia, you've got to, mate! You've got to!" Mikki said, getting all fired up.

"It couldn't hurt," Sivya said. "The worst thing that could happen is you lose an arm."

"Hello," Georgia said. "How?"

"From typing?" Sivya shrugged. "See? It's a risk worth taking."

"That's all fine and dandy and hippy-dippy, but what am I supposed to write about all of a sudden? It's the 'New Faces in Fashion' issue and I've got nothing."

"Alexa's a new face in fashion," Sivya pointed out. "I mean, isn't she?"

"Totally," Mikki said.

"Most definitely," Shawn added.

"Oh, no," Alexa said, laughing lightly. But it was too late.

It was her idea, Georgia thought. "You don't think you're getting away so easily now, do you?"

Alexa glanced at Shawn. "*Ay,* what did I get myself into?"

"An interview," Georgia said, scrambling in her desk drawer for a tape recorder. "An in-depth, probing interview." She grinned. "Get ready to bare your soul,

Alexa Veron. I don't know if you've heard the rumors, but I'm ruthless."

@ @ @ @

The interview went smoothly. Alexa was a fascinating subject—she said she loved modeling, but loved being a photographer more. She would soon juggle both when she went to a fine arts school in New York. "It may not be possible," Alexa said in the interview. "I may have to choose one over the other. And then, *ay*, trouble."

"Oh, I'm sure you can do both," Georgia said with authority. *Not that I really know. I'm just hoping such a thing might be possible. For my own selfish sake.*

After the interview was over and Alexa went back to the Beauty department for her shoot—the whole reason she was there at *Flirt* that day—Georgia tried to write at her desk. But she kept getting interrupted: The Entertainment eds wanted copies made and, on top of that, Ms. Bishop couldn't find Elizabeth and wanted Georgia to send a fax.

Can't they see I have real work to do?!

Georgia slunk away from her cubicle into the back hallway. She saw a sign that said STAIRWAY and entered. She went as far up as she could go, until she reached the topmost door in the stairwell. It came open to the rooftop. If she ignored the bulky, rusted air-conditioning units and other ugly machinery that did who knew what and looked past it all to the skyline, she had a view of Manhattan like no other.

Huh, she thought. *I should bring a chair up here.*

She found a comfortable, basically clean spot on the ledge and pulled out her trusty Sidekick. She was a master with those itty-bitty keys. And so, high up in the haze of smog hovering over midtown, she started writing.

ⓖ ⓖ ⓖ ⓖ

Oh no! Georgia screamed-thought later that night. *No, no, no, oh please, no!*

She felt like she was in the midst of a scene from a slasher film and the director had told her to be "in the moment." She was so "in the moment," she was running out of her room and to the spiral staircase shrieking.

Some of the other interns were on the couches in the living room. On hearing Georgia, they bolted upright, alarmed.

"Is there a fire?" Nailah said, heading to the telephone.

"No!" Georgia said. It wasn't a natural disaster, it was worse. Georgia couldn't get her Alexa Veron article off her Sidekick and onto her computer. It was catastrophic. "I have a virus!" Georgia announced dramatically from the top of the stairs.

Asha looked up, stricken. "I cannot get ill," she said. "I have too much to do."

"Not that kind of a virus. A computer virus, or a Sidekick virus. Sivya, you've got to save me, like now."

Sivya laughed outright. "So no need to call the fire department?"

Georgia shook her head. "My computer won't download my article. It's infected, I know it."

Nailah sat back down on the couch, completely unconcerned. Sivya shrugged. "You have a Mac, Georgia. It's next to impossible for you to have a virus. Are you sure you have your USB cable plugged in?"

Georgia shot her a deadly look. "Fix it, Sivya!" Then she added, "Pretty please?"

Sivya saluted crookedly and made a big show of leaping off the couch.

"We should get you a fancy cape," Mikki said. "Our techie superhero. First you save Lizzy, now you rescue Georgia . . ."

Sivya waved the compliment away. "Lizzy didn't really need saving," she said. "Where is she, anyway?"

"She's with Nova," Mikki said. She seemed a little miffed about it. "They're meeting some of Nova's mates, or whatevs."

"Didn't she say she had a lot of work to do this weekend?" Asha said.

"Who cares about Lizzy's stupid book deal and her

feature article and the fact that she has the best hair out of all of us?" Georgia shrieked.

"What?" Asha said.

Mikki pulled on one of her own wild curls. "Hey, I happen to *like* my hair, mate."

"C'mon, Georgia," Sivya said. "Let's check out your laptop and see what's wrong." She turned back to Mikki. "I like your hair, too."

They went upstairs to Georgia's laptop in the bedroom. It sat open on the desk by the window. Sivya sat before it, her fingers poised over the keys. "You just want to get whatever's on your Sidekick onto your hard drive, am I right?" she asked.

Georgia nodded, waving her arms. "Whatever the fancy language is, yeah."

Sivya clicked a few options in a preferences window. "Georgia, you were just using your software improperly. I told you there was no virus. See?"

All her files and e-mails started downloading. Georgia's e-mail program was open, and suddenly a list of e-mails started showing up, one after another, all to the same recipient: *Stalkerazzi, Stalkerazzi, Stalkerazzi.*

Sivya looked confused. "What's all that?" she asked.

"It's nothing," Georgia said. "Just make it stop. I just need my article."

But Sivya was more than curious now. There were

dozens of e-mails to Stalkerazzi.com, and they all appeared to be from Georgia. There were others, too, to a guy called Joey Joey—so many that the screen filled up with them and kept going, the downloads seeming endless. Snippets could be seen of the e-mails:

I'll be at BED @ 10 tonite. —G

Going out for Red Bull. Corner of Spring & Greene. —G

Got audition for new Mirra movie. Details to come. —G

No, was all Georgia could think, the voice in her head no longer coherent. Without warning, she reached out and slammed her laptop shut.

Sivya slowly turned to her with giant eyes.

"That's not what it looks like," Georgia said.

She felt a range of emotions, so many she had no clue how she must have looked. She was panicked. She was scared. She wanted to laugh; maybe that was nerves. And she was mortified, absolutely mortified. Now Sivya knew she was an attention whore. And a pathetic one at that. No use denying it now.

Sivya swallowed. Carefully she said, "Um, Georgia? What it looks like is that you've been tipping off the paparazzi this whole time."

"So maybe it is what it looks like, but—"

All at once there was a great amount of shrieking in the hallway just outside the room. Both Sivya and Georgia jumped and went to the door. Nova and Elizabeth had come back with a bunch of Nova's friends in tow. They were all climbing up the ladder to the roof. Mikki ran by. "You mates coming? Nova brought the party home tonight."

Sivya shrugged. "Your computer's fine, Georgia," she said. She gave her a look, and Georgia knew she wouldn't say anything, as usual.

I'll just have to be really, really nice to Sivya. Buy her that Prada gown or something. Wait—is this party on the roof? MY roof?

Georgia ran for the ladder. "Don't let them sit in my chair!" she yelled. She reached the rooftop to find Nova and four friends, plus Mikki and Elizabeth and—no way!—a cooler full of beer.

"You can't have those up here, you know," Georgia said, standing there with her hands on her hips.

Sivya came up behind her and added, "If Emma finds out, you guys'll get into so much trouble. She's still mad about curfew."

"Want one?" one of Nova's friends asked Sivya. "Hey, I like your shirt. D'you skate?" He was clearly a skater boy: baggy pants, huge T-shirt with some kind of alien head on the front, cap on sideways, and a spiked leather band around his wrist.

Sivya actually glanced around to see if he was talking to someone else. She was dressed pretty much the same as he was, like she'd raided his closet. "I can skate," she said shyly. She headed for the cooler. "Sure. I'll have a little, I guess."

"You cannot be serious!" Georgia said.

Nova narrowed her eyes. "Georgia, you're being totally uncool. Emma's not here. She won't find out. So take it down a notch and chill, okay?"

"Yeah," Elizabeth added from beside the cooler. "Chill, Georgia." The words sounded ridiculous coming from her mouth.

"How's your book coming, Lizzy?" Georgia found herself saying, surprised at the level of animosity. "How're you gonna write it if you're drunk?"

"Who said anything about getting drunk? God," Nova said. She was so done with this conversation, she turned her back on Georgia and started talking to her friends.

"I finished," Elizabeth said. She took a sip of her beer.

"You finished your book?" *What is she, the best writer in the world AND the fastest?*

"I got inspired," Elizabeth said. She shot a smile at Mikki. "I wrote some chapters, not the whole book, but enough to give my agent, so I'm not worried." She leaned back in her lawn chair. Georgia noticed suddenly how her appearance had changed in the last week. She'd gone from preppy collared Izod shirts to a skinny-strapped tank top. And her hair had lost its barrettes.

"Whatever," Georgia said.

"And I've got you to thank," Elizabeth said.

"Me?" Georgia said. "For what?"

"You inspired me," Elizabeth said. "You're so"— she searched for the word—"you're such a character, Georgia."

"A *what*?" Georgia was getting steamed.

Nova turned back, smiling lightly. "She's right," she said. "You totally are."

"I'm a person! I'm a human being!" Georgia said. She noticed that Nova's friends were laughing at her, and it made everything so much worse. "It's not funny," she said.

Sivya gave her a goofy look and shrugged. "I think she means it as a compliment, Georgia," she said.

"Are you writing your book about me?" Georgia said.

"Maybe a little," Elizabeth said.

"That would be some novel," Mikki said. "Is Georgia the bad guy or the good guy?"

"Don't answer that," Georgia said. She was about to pitch a fit, maybe start throwing things, when it occurred to her: Elizabeth said she wasn't writing about her, but if she was inspired by her, Georgia had to be in there somewhere.

And Georgia was going to take this opportunity to find out. "You know what?" she said. "I'm flattered."

"Really?" Elizabeth said.

"Yeah," Georgia said through clenched teeth. "*So* flattered."

"Cool," Elizabeth said.

"I'm gonna go downstairs. Work on my, um"—she glanced at Sivya, willing her to keep her mouth shut about the tip-offs—"some stuff."

"You don't want to stay up here and party?" Nova asked. "You can go wild and the paparazzi won't see. Unless they have helicopters?" Everyone looked up at the sky.

"Nah," Georgia said. "But you guys have fun. You can use my chair if you want." She waved toward the umbrella-blanket contraption on the other side of the roof. "It's super comfortable." She was acting really generous; she just hoped everyone bought it.

Because once down the ladder, she snuck straight into the bedroom Elizabeth shared with Mikki and Sivya and closed the door. She headed for Elizabeth's laptop on her bed, popped it open, and turned it on. She was going to find out for herself just what exactly Elizabeth's supposedly brilliant novel said about her. If she was the bad guy, she wanted to know now. Then she'd call her lawyer and sue.

But as she sat on the edge of Elizabeth's bed,

waiting for her computer to boot up, she felt something lumpy under the mattress. Weird. Elizabeth had jammed a ton of magazines between her two mattresses, like she was hiding something trashy. Georgia reached in and pulled them out. They had *Flirt* Library stickers on them.

Contraband! Georgia thought. But it wasn't anything illegal. Ooooh, she swiped a few magazines. So what.

She dumped the magazines on the floor and started searching through Elizabeth's hard disk. She was looking for a folder called "Novel" or, even better, "Ideas I Stole from Georgia Cooper," or something like that.

But her attention returned to the magazines. One was folded open to a page. In bright red, yellow, and green letters it said: "My First Trip to Mexico."

Isn't her article for the "New Faces" issue about Mexico?

Georgia reached down and picked it up. It was just some random article by some random person in some tiny, little, totally random magazine no one's ever heard of. She was about to drop it back on the floor when something in the article caught her eye. A line. Then a whole paragraph.

This is almost exactly like Elizabeth's article, Georgia thought, sort of numb. She checked the byline again. It was written by someone named Aly Madchen. Most definitely not Elizabeth Cheekwood.

"No way," Georgia said out loud.

She heard a sound in the hallway and froze. Was someone coming in? But no—it was just someone passing by, probably Nailah or Asha on their way up to join the party.

Georgia started sifting through Elizabeth's hard drive for something else. When she found it—the article Elizabeth had turned in to Ms. Bishop just that morning—she completely forgot about Elizabeth's novel that was maybe about her, maybe not.

Elizabeth had copied this other writer's story. Some of the lines were hers, and some were changed just enough to make them different, but others were exactly like what this Aly Madchen had written. Unless Elizabeth Cheekwood had written the first Mexico article under a pseudonym, this was out-and-out plagiarism.

This was huge.

Georgia froze, stunned. *I KNEW IT,* she thought defiantly. Her spirits soared. Then they came to a sudden halt and smacked back down to earth. *But what am I supposed to do now?*

ⓖ   ⓖ   ⓖ   ⓖ

"Come in," Ms. Bishop called from inside her office.

Georgia gathered her courage and stepped in. It was Monday morning. In one hand was the magazine containing Aly Madchen's article. In the other hand were a few pages, her own story that she'd slaved over all weekend. She was shaking.

But she had to do it.

She had to.

She had—

"Georgia, you said you needed to see me, so what is it?"

"I have to talk to you," Georgia said.

"Then talk," Ms. Bishop said. She seemed even more impatient than usual.

The woman is editor-in-chief and publisher of a magazine empire, don't forget! Does she want to see your piddly article? No, she does not.

But she will want to know about Elizabeth.

Georgia began talking before she could stop herself. It was like she was channeling some confident other part of herself. Acting, you might say.

"I know the deadline was Friday, but I wrote something new this weekend," Georgia said. She pushed her Alexa Veron article across the desk.

Ms. Bishop skimmed it. "You interviewed one of the previous interns, I see."

"Yes. But not because she was an intern. She's an up-and-coming model, and I believe she'll one day also be a fashion photographer. She'd be perfect for the 'New Faces in Fashion' issue."

"I'll consider it," Ms. Bishop said. "Although I'm not sure if there's any room left. But I do appreciate your tenacity. Also, I have good news: We just hired the new Entertainment editor. Her name is Jane Wolander, and she starts next week."

"Oh, that's great," Georgia said, her voice sounding a little flat. She knew Jane. She should be happy that she got to work with Jane.

But what would Jane think about what she was about to do?

Ms. Bishop's smile faltered. "I thought you'd be thrilled to have a mentor at last."

"I am," Georgia said. Then she started talking and she couldn't stop. "About my article . . . I do think there will be room to publish it if you think it's worthy. Because I doubt you'd want a tired old article by some nobody called Elizabeth Cheekwood when you could have a real original piece by Georgia Cooper." Her voice wavered only a little. "Besides, I wrote my article all by myself, which is more than I can say for Elizabeth."

Ms. Bishop's interest was immediately piqued. "Explain," she commanded.

What am I doing? Why do I have to be the one to tell her?

But she was the one who knew. And it was wrong, it wasn't fair, and someone had to tell her. Even if it made Georgia the bad guy, she knew it was the right thing to do.

"I found this," Georgia said. She placed the magazine on the desk, the one with the article written by Aly Madchen. She opened it to the incriminating page. "It sounds a lot like Elizabeth's article. But someone else wrote it."

Ms. Bishop began reading. A grim look settled on her face. Half of Georgia wanted to sink into the plush carpet and disappear. The other half wanted to stand firm and demand that her own article be published in its place. There was no going back now.

"Where did you get this?" Ms. Bishop said.

"I found it," Georgia said. "In Elizabeth's room."

Ms. Bishop reached forward and pressed a button on her telephone console. "Delia, get Quinn in here immediately."

Georgia stood there, waiting. Would they call her a snoop for digging this up? Would they think she'd somehow been involved?

"Georgia, is there anything else?" Ms. Bishop snapped.

"No," Georgia said so quietly she could hardly hear herself.

"Then go. We'll handle this. It's no longer any of your concern."

Georgia didn't hesitate. She left Ms. Bishop's office and returned to her desk in a daze. She stared at

66 There was no going back now. 99

her computer for a full minute before realizing that there was a dancing character on her screen, that bouncing pigtailed cartoon girl. Kiyoko was haunting her from the intern grave again.

Sivya poked her head over the cubicle wall. "Um, Georgia, could you turn your speakers down? It's really loud."

Georgia was so out of it she didn't even realize that music was blaring from her computer. It was a strange electronic mix, like nothing she'd ever heard. "It's that Kiyoko freak," Georgia said. "She's done something to the computer again."

Sivya came around and immediately hit the MUTE key. A balloon appeared near the animated character's head.

Time to say congratulations! the speech balloon announced. Balloons kept popping up.

You've made it through yr first 2 weeks.
And if you're still here to read this, then . . .
You've earned the right to call yourself
my successor!

The pigtailed character on screen stuck out her tongue and blew a raspberry.

"So weird," Sivya said.

Then another balloon bounced on the screen:

Now the madness starts. Look in the
mirror, new intern. 'Cause you won't

recognize yo' bad self by summer's end.
Love ya 4-eva! —KIYoKO Katsuda, intern of
the gods

"Yikes," Sivya said. "What does she think's going to happen, anyway?"

"Who knows," Georgia said quietly.

"She'd better watch what she says to you. It could end up all over the Web."

Georgia shot her a look.

"Just kidding," Sivya said. She returned to her cube. Georgia watched the pigtailed Kiyoko do one final dance and then turn into a million little bubbles and fade away. It was over. The computer was hers again.

Kiyoko seemed to know that some big things were about to happen and that they'd change her forever.

Kiyoko, she thought, *you have no idea.*

ⓖ　　ⓖ　　ⓖ　　ⓖ

Monday ended like any other day. Georgia had no idea what had happened between Ms. Bishop and Elizabeth. She'd avoided Elizabeth for the rest of the day and returned to the loft on her own, skipping out early to catch a cab to SoHo instead of taking the subway with the other girls.

The cab stopped at her curb. It was only when she

was searching her Fendi purse for extra bills for a tip that she noticed the guy on the corner: Tyler, her messenger cutie, standing astride his bike. When she stepped out of the cab, he raised his arm to wave. He'd been waiting for her. *What's he doing downtown?* she thought, waving back. He didn't have any packages.

Then she realized what was going on. Running into Tyler hadn't been accidental, oh no. Now here he was again, at the loft where she lived (!), and how would he have gotten ahold of her address? He'd been following her. He probably had a hidden camera on his bike, a wire taped to the muscled chest under his shirt—*do not think of his chest, Georgia!* What dirt was he trying to dig up about her? And who was he selling it to?

That was *it*. She marched up to him. "So who do you work for?" she demanded.

"Roadrunner Messenger Service"—he lifted his messenger bag to show the logo—"you know that." He was grinning and it showed in his eyes, bright hazel, their warm light pulling her in. The dimple was back.

Georgia looked away. "Really," she said. Her Molly Mack mystery-solving skills were reemerging. How could she have been so clueless? "Then what are you doing here? And don't tell me you were 'delivering a package.' I know the truth."

"And what is the truth?" he prompted, still grinning.

"The truth is . . ." *You're really cute.* "You followed me, didn't you? I may be from Hollywood, but I'm not dumb."

He held up his hands in surrender. "You got me," he said. "How'd you guess?"

"It's obvious. So how much are they paying you?"

A look of confusion flickered over his face. "Roadrunner, you mean?"

"Huh?"

They stood looking at each other, equally confused.

"Are you following me for a newspaper or what?" she said at last.

"I saw you in the taxi outside the Hudson-Bennett building, and my shift is over, so I just followed the cab down Broadway."

"Oh god." Georgia covered her face, hiding under her hands for a few seconds. When she reemerged, he was still standing there, balancing his bike on the curb, the grin back on his face. "I'm such a dope," she said. "I thought . . ."

"You thought I was, what? Selling smack on you to the tabloids?"

She swallowed, didn't utter an answer, but she knew he knew. "Sorry," she said. "Forgive me?"

"Let me think," he said. He scuffed the toe of his sneaker against the pavement. She noted that one of his pant legs was rolled up again, just the one. Finally, he lifted his eyes to hers as if he'd made his decision. She liked the suspense. "I'll forgive you," he said. "On one condition."

"Which is . . . ?"

"Give me your number. We'll do something this weekend. No bikes involved."

"I don't mind the bike," she said.

"Is that a yes?"

In answer, she reached into her Fendi purse and scrawled her number on the back of the taxi receipt. "That's my cell," she said. "My direct number."

She never gave out her direct number. Did he realize the significance of that?

He took it and put it in his pocket. Then he reached for her hand. She didn't know what he would do: Inspect it for dirt? Suck on her knuckle? Eat the opal out of her ring?

But he did The Weirdest Thing Ever. He held her hand to his lips, looking at her for a moment. Then he kissed her hand, *kissed it*! She didn't know boys still did that.

"Oh," she said under her breath. She had no idea what else to say now, or do. Oddly enough, it was the most romantic thing that had ever happened to her in her sixteen years on this planet. And she'd dated Anton Stone, who'd been voted the number-seven fantasy date in a

Tiger Beat survey. With that one kiss (not even technically a kiss), Tyler had Anton beat, no doubt.

And that's when the flash blinded her. She blinked, and Tyler said "What's that?" and it kept up—*flash, flash, flash*—and Tyler let her hand go. Her arm fell back to her side, tingling with electricity.

She sought out the camera. Behind it was a tie-dyed shirt.

"Georgia!" Joey Joey called. "Who's your friend?"

"Beautiful," she snapped. This was not the time to be stalked by paparazzi.

"So I'll call you," Tyler said awkwardly, hopping on his bike.

"Don't let the cameras stop you," Georgia said. She watched him hop the curb and ride north out of SoHo. Then she turned on Joey Joey, her hands balled into fists.

"Yikes," Joey Joey said.

ⓖ　　ⓖ　　ⓖ　　ⓖ

Georgia was in her chair on the rooftop, hiding out from the rest of the girls. She sat under the umbrella, her heart still beating. She felt on top of the world.

What a day.

Then she noticed a pair of feet approaching her chair, and her heart stopped moving in her chest. What a day was right—and it wasn't over. The two feet belonged

"You can see right through me."

to Elizabeth, and here was the part of the day where Elizabeth got her revenge.

"Hi," Elizabeth said. She sat on the ledge before Georgia's chair.

Georgia was expecting Elizabeth to start yelling. *Wait for it . . .*

But Elizabeth only stretched and let out a big yawn. "I'm exhausted," she said. "I don't think I slept more than four hours last night."

Georgia made an indeterminate sound in her throat.

"Yeah, I had coffee and everything," Elizabeth said.

Georgia sat up straighter in her chair. "Is this really what you came up here to tell me, how tired you are and how you had coffee? Or did you want to say something else?"

Just out with it. Give me a chance to defend myself. I'm ready. Sort of.

Elizabeth flushed. "You can see right through me," she said. Then she produced some pages from behind her back. "Listen, Georgia, I came up here to show you these. I wasn't being exactly honest with you before. So I wanted you to read something."

"I know, Lizzy," Georgia said. "I already read it."

"You read my novel already? How? I haven't shown these chapters to anyone yet, except for my agent. And she hasn't even e-mailed me back yet to say what she thinks."

"This is your novel?" Georgia said. She took a closer look. She didn't see anything about Mexico.

"I started over," Elizabeth said. "It's a completely different book now. I hope my agent's not upset."

"Why are you showing me this?"

"You'll see."

Georgia started reading. Just from the first paragraph, she could see that the story was somewhat—okay, blatantly—about her. The narrator had long red hair and bright green eyes. She was from Hollywood. She was a child actress. She said "beautiful" a lot, and most of the time it was not genuine.

"You *are* writing about me," Georgia said.

"Yeah," Elizabeth said. "I meant it when I said you inspired me. My novel used to be about this adventurous girl who'd been, like, all over the world and done all these incredible things. She was supposed to be me. But she so wasn't me. I've never done anything. I've never even been off the East Coast."

I know, Lizzy. I know.

Georgia swallowed heavily. *She has no idea what I told Ms. Bishop.*

Elizabeth continued. "So I started thinking about

you, and all the things you've done, and I guess I started writing about your life, Georgia, or how I imagined it would be, and I couldn't stop. I want to change my whole novel."

"Wow," Georgia said.

"Read it, then tell me what you think. I swear it's not mean or anything. And it's fiction. I didn't steal anything."

Georgia froze in her lounge chair. *Now that you mention stealing . . .*

She had to do it. She had to come clean. And this was her shot, now, when they were alone up on the rooftop. Georgia put the pages of Elizabeth's novel aside. "I'll read it later, I promise," she said. "I'm glad you came up here."

"Oh, so am I, Georgia. I was nervous to tell you, but I—"

"Elizabeth." Elizabeth stopped talking, seeing something in Georgia's eyes. Georgia went on. "I'm glad you came up here because there's something I need to say to you, too." She took a breath. "Did Ms. Bishop talk to you today?"

"Not really," Elizabeth said. "She seemed super busy. Why?"

"You're going to hate me," Georgia said. Then she gathered up all her courage and confessed what she did.

chapter eight

Elizabeth listened in a daze.

". . . so I showed that magazine to her, I had to, and she read it, and she didn't say what she'd do, but, well, I guess she'll tell you." Georgia paused. "And also, while we're at it, that stuff I said about Ms. Bishop liking Melanie Henderson better than you . . . I sort of made that up. It's not true. I have no idea who she likes or doesn't like. That woman's a mystery, for real."

Elizabeth's throat felt dry, her tongue a slab of concrete. She just sat there.

"Say something," Georgia prompted.

"I—I can't." No lie, not this time.

"Say something about what?" someone butted in. It was Mikki. "You have *got* to come downstairs, you two. Right now, mates! It's urgent!"

Mikki dragged Elizabeth and Georgia off the rooftop. Downstairs, Sivya had brought back a magazine layout from the "New Faces" issue, still in progress. She kept it hidden behind her back, building up the excitement.

Elizabeth and Georgia separated and stood far apart from each other.

"What I have here is the table of contents," Sivya was announcing as the girls gathered around. "Trey's letting me design it all by myself. I'll show you guys if you promise me two things. Do not—I repeat—*do not* tell Trey that I printed out a copy to bring back here."

"Why?" Asha's eyes widened in alarm. "Are you not supposed to have it?"

"Where did you get it?" Nailah asked at the same time.

"I didn't steal anything!" Sivya shrieked. "What do you guys think I am?"

Elizabeth felt herself jump. She wanted to slip away. She wanted to call her parents, but tell them what?

I messed up. You're not going to believe what I did, but . . .

I stole someone else's story and pretended it was mine.

She couldn't say that. Sometimes it was easier to pretend a thing wasn't happening than to face it head on.

Someone was elbowing her in the ribs: Mikki. "Aren't you stoked? Don't you want to see your name on that table of contents, mate?"

Elizabeth nodded. She did want to see her name there. And she knew she wouldn't.

"Just get on with it," Nova called to Sivya. "What's the other thing you want us to promise?"

"That you won't laugh at me," Sivya said.

" *Aren't you stoked? Don't you want to see your name on that table of contents, mate?* **"**

"Why on earth would we laugh at you?" Asha asked.

"I'd laugh," Mikki said, shrugging, "if it happened to be funny."

Sivya stuck her tongue out at Mikki. "I just mean . . . this is my first design project. I never had a chance to be creative before. So if it sucks—"

"We'll pretend it doesn't," Nova said impatiently. "Just show us already."

Sivya didn't move. Elizabeth held her breath.

"Oh, I get it," Mikki teased. "It's all black and gray, isn't it?"

"Black and gray would be cool," Nova said. "C'mon, Sivya, honestly. Knowing you, I bet it's awesome."

Sivya slowly unfurled a surprisingly colorful page from behind her back and the girls leaped on her, crowding around to see. Both Elizabeth and Georgia hung back, eyeing each other over the other girls' backs. By the squeals and screams, it soon became clear whose names were listed in the table of contents:

Asha! Her modified lip-stain recipe was noted in the Beauty section.

Mikki! One of her collage illustrations appeared.

Nailah! A sports-injury piece she'd drawn up was featured.

And Georgia! Her article on Alexa Veron was listed in the Entertainment section.

"Congratulations, Georgia," Elizabeth said so quietly she could barely hear herself.

Everyone was looking at her.

"Can I just say something?" Mikki spoke up. "I am shocked. S-H-O-C-K-E-D, shocked. I thought for sure Ms. Bishop would pick your article, Lizzy."

"I thought you were a shoo-in," Asha said. "Maybe it's a mistake?"

"It's not a mistake," Elizabeth said. Her voice was all gravelly.

"I'm sorry!" Sivya burst out. She bounded over to give Elizabeth a hug, but Elizabeth pulled away before she could stop herself. The words were on the edge of her lips. *I have something to tell you.*

"I have some news," Nailah broke in. "My boss, Gayle, told me. I don't think the other supervisors have made the announcement as of yet."

"What? They don't like us and want all new interns?" Nova said.

Asha looked horrified.

"Joking," Nova said.

"You girls have all watched the *Flirt It!* reality show,

"That was my agent. I got the part."

yes?" Nailah said.

"Adonia is so gonna win," Sivya said.

"No way," Nova said. "I'd put cold hard cash on Svetlana."

"What about the show, Nailah?" Asha prompted.

"It seems that we're all to be working on it. Next week. Gayle had me calling some of the local gyms to set up personal trainers for the two finalists."

"Are they coming to New York? We get to meet them?" Sivya said.

Nailah shrugged. "It seems so."

"I love this summer," Sivya said. "Could it get any better? I mean, could it?"

Then a phone started ringing. Georgia popped open her cell and stepped over to a window seat to have her conversation.

"If that's Anton Stone coming for a Hollywood-themed slumber party, I might keel over," Mikki said, fanning herself dramatically beside Sivya.

Now Georgia was coming back to the other girls, a stunned look on her face. "That was my agent," she said. "I got the part. In the Esteban Mirra movie. No joke."

"Congrats, Georgia!" Sivya squealed, wrapping her in a tight hug. Georgia looked choked, but handled it well enough. "Wait, wow, what does that mean?"

"Georgia," Nova said, "you're up for an Esteban Mirra movie? Since when?"

"Yeah, when did this happen?" Asha said.

"It happened," Georgia said, not giving any other details. "And I guess they start shooting this month. In Toronto."

"I thought you said the movie was set in New York City," Sivya said.

"It is, but a lot of movies about New York are shot in Toronto," Georgia said.

"So what are you going to do, then?" Asha asked. "You can't be in New York and Toronto at the same time."

Georgia shrugged. "I don't know. I guess I've got a big decision to make. But I doubt you guys'll miss me if I leave."

"What?" Sivya said. "We love you, Georgia!" None of the other girls followed suit. Apparently Georgia had made one true friend in the past two weeks, and that was Sivya. All the other girls mumbled agreement but conveniently looked away toward other spots in the room. "I would miss you," Sivya insisted.

"I hope you don't have to leave," Elizabeth said to Georgia. She meant it, too.

"Yeah, what Lizzy said," Mikki added.

Elizabeth locked her gaze on Georgia's. She waited

for Georgia to say something to the other girls—to out her, to tell them all what she did—but Georgia said nothing.

ⓖ ⠀⠀ ⓖ ⠀⠀ ⓖ ⠀⠀ ⓖ

From: cgack@gackliteraryagency.com
To: elizabeth_cheekwood@webdotmail.com
Re: Your new chapters

Elizabeth,

We really must talk. I've been having trouble reaching you by phone. I admit I'm confused by the chapters you sent. Is this the same book? The character is completely different. The voice is strong, but not at all what it was before. Elizabeth, you're giving me doubts that we can sustain a long narrative. I do hope that this novel isn't too much pressure on you at such a young age. Although, knowing you, I'm sure you can assure me otherwise.

Let's chat. I'll be in the office until 4:30.
All best, Connie

Tuesday morning, Elizabeth was at her desk at *Flirt*. She read her literary agent's e-mail again and again. She wasn't in the mood to "chat" about the doubts her agent was having over her new chapters. That was because she had another e-mail. And this one was even more alarming:

From: delia_z@flirt.com
To: elizabeth_c@flirt.com
Re: Urgent matter

Ms. Bishop wants you in her office at 10. —Delia

Elizabeth had a terrible feeling. She was trying to come up with viable excuses, something, anything that would make sense to a woman like Ms. Bishop. How could Elizabeth coherently explain her panic at all the work she needed to get done? Plus wanting the chance to see the city and just have fun? Was that even worth saying?

Elizabeth put her head down on her desk. She wanted to stay there until it was time for the meeting, but someone thumped her on the back. She jumped.

"Mate!" Mikki exclaimed.

Elizabeth looked in Mikki's freckled face, a smudge of blue paint on her chin as if she'd gotten up at sunrise that morning, inspired. Probably she had. Elizabeth pointed to Mikki's chin. "You've got something—" she started.

"Cerulean," Mikki said. "I knew it. Come with." Mikki pulled Elizabeth into the ladies' room with her. As she scrubbed the spot from her chin, she gave Elizabeth a probing look in the mirror. "So what's the matter?"

It's nothing. Everything's fine.

No, that wouldn't work. Mikki was a real friend. Only the truth would work.

"I made a mistake," Elizabeth started. "A huge mistake."

"What, like a typo?" Mikki said.

Elizabeth shook her head. Mikki's chin was clean. "You know that article I turned in, the one about Mexico?"

"Yeah, so?"

"I've never been to Mexico, Mikki."

Mikki cocked her head, confused. "So it's fiction, then? You made it up?"

"Not exactly. I copied it. Parts of it." She didn't know how to explain it, so it all tumbled out, the article she found in the magazine, the way she started typing her own article with that article next to it, the way the sentences became her sentences, the way it somehow seemed all right at the time. It had seemed to make sense, until the next day, when she turned the article in with her name on it and it was too late to go back.

Mikki's face was stricken. "Lizzy, that's so not good. When Bishop finds out . . ."

"She knows already. Georgia told her."

"What?" Mikki looked about to have a heart attack. "Georgia told on you?"

"I have to go. Ms. Bishop wants to meet with me at ten." She started for the door, but Mikki's hand on her arm kept her in place.

"Lizzy . . ."

"What you must think of me," Elizabeth said, unable to even face her friend.

"Lizzy, why didn't you tell me you needed help?"

"I never need help. I can handle everything, always, I guess." Elizabeth took a breath and pulled her arm out of Mikki's grasp. "Until now."

🌀   🌀   🌀   🌀

"We have a no-tolerance policy for plagiarism," Ms. Bishop said. The look on her face was cold.

Elizabeth couldn't believe this was happening. Except that it *was* happening: It was only the start of her third week in New York and she was sitting across from Ms. Bishop in her giant, gleaming office overlooking Times Square, about to get into the most serious trouble of her entire life. The managing editor, Quinn, was also in the room, sitting quietly beside Elizabeth, witness to her mortification.

At first she'd thought of excuses: *I didn't mean to. It just happened. I was really stressed and didn't want to disappoint anyone.*

Then she kept recalling Mikki's face in the bathroom—how shocked she'd looked, like it was the last thing on earth she'd think of doing, copying another person's work and calling it her own.

"Ms. Bishop, Mr. Carson"—Elizabeth took a deep

breath and forged on—"I can't say enough how sorry I am. I'm terribly sorry. I'm so embarrassed. I know I was wrong. I never should have let the pressure get to me. I made a terrible, awful mistake."

"Elizabeth, do you understand what a no-tolerance policy is?" Ms. Bishop asked.

A bad feeling hit Elizabeth's gut. There was the faintest of sounds in the room, the hush of the air conditioner and little else. "Yes," she said. "I know you won't be publishing the article."

"Of course we won't be publishing the article," Quinn said.

Ms. Bishop eyed Quinn and he closed his mouth.

"I made a terrible mistake in judgment," Elizabeth said. "I'll never do it again."

"No," Ms. Bishop said, "you won't." She shook her head. "This is the last thing I expected of you, Elizabeth, a girl with your talent." Elizabeth started to open her mouth to speak, to say thank you or something, but Ms. Bishop kept going, and what she said next was even worse. "I've called your parents myself. I had a long talk with your mother. She's arriving today so you can fly back together. We've made arrangements for you to leave the loft tomorrow morning."

Elizabeth could hardly think coherently, let alone talk. "I . . . I don't understand. You're sending me home?" It came out like a question and hung in the air for a moment before Ms. Bishop answered with a nod of her head.

This, Elizabeth wasn't expecting. She thought she'd get a second chance. A punishment, a month slaving over the fax, lose the chance to have a story published in *Flirt*, something awful for sure, but not this!

"That's what a no-tolerance policy means, Elizabeth," Ms. Bishop said. "It means your internship is over. You'll have the night to say good-bye to your friends. I wish you the best, I do." She stood up. "Quinn, have you arranged for the car service?"

Quinn nodded. "Jared's waiting for you downstairs," he told Elizabeth, his voice softer than it was before.

"It's really over?" Elizabeth found herself asking. She was still holding onto the hope that Ms. Bishop would have a change of heart.

Ms. Bishop nodded, seeming sad about it but also resigned. "Yes," she said.

Elizabeth took a step for the door. "Thank you for this opportunity, Ms. Bishop. I'm sorry I let you down." Then she left the room.

ⓖ   ⓖ   ⓖ   ⓖ

Elizabeth heard the girls come in downstairs, but she stayed in her room, folding her clothes neatly into her suitcase. She heard them banging around, dropping their things on the couch, talking. She dreaded the moment when the first of the girls would come up the stairs and try to talk to her. She'd already had a long talk with Emma, who had been warned of her early departure and was there waiting when she'd arrived back at the loft. She'd also talked to her mother on the phone, who had been rushing to catch her flight at the airport, and whose disappointment was palpable even in the few hurried minutes they spoke.

What will the other girls say to me? Elizabeth thought. Because if this had happened to any of the other interns—if they'd done something so bad as to get themselves kicked out of the program—she wouldn't have known what to say. She probably would have avoided talking to the girl as long as she could, which may have been why no one was climbing the stairs looking for her.

She put the last of her clothes in the suitcase. Then she went to the hallway, just out of sight, and listened to what was going on downstairs.

They were fighting.

"But how could you do it? You didn't talk to her first! You had to go straight to her boss!" That was Mikki. Elizabeth had never heard her sound so upset.

"We could have done something, I bet. Like catch the story before Ms. Bishop read it, maybe?" Sivya said. "I don't know."

"I know why," Nova said. "She wanted her story in the 'New Faces' issue. Isn't that right, Georgia? It's all about you."

They were ganging up on Georgia. "I'm not the one who plagiarized," Elizabeth heard Georgia say. "Why are you guys mad at me?"

"Because you used this for your own personal gain," Nova said. "You just wanted to look good in front of Ms. Bishop. You're a kiss-up."

"Because you're so selfish and Lizzy's my friend and now she has to go home and it didn't have to be this way, I know it." Mikki again. Elizabeth was touched at how she was defending her—when, really, what she did was indefensible.

"She stole someone else's story! Are you all idiots?!" Georgia was now shrieking.

Elizabeth stepped out of the hallway and toward the stairs, where the other girls could see her. "Georgia's right," she said.

The girls froze. Everyone was down there—even Asha and Nailah, standing off to the side, watching with drawn expressions.

Elizabeth went downstairs to join them. "I'm not mad at Georgia," she said. "I know she told Ms. Bishop, but I'm not mad. You all have seen how hard Georgia's been working these past couple weeks. She's serious about this internship, and what I did just showed that I wasn't. She

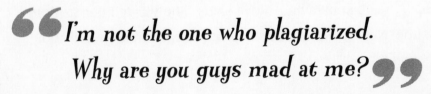
I'm not the one who plagiarized.
Why are you guys mad at me?

didn't do what she did to look good for anyone, I know it."

"Thanks," Georgia said.

"Is this a joke?" Nova said. "Georgia wants people to pay attention only to her. Ms. Bishop liked you, so she fixed it. She couldn't handle the competition."

"I don't think that's the reason," Elizabeth said. Georgia wouldn't meet her eyes.

Nova nudged Sivya. "Tell them," she said.

Sivya blushed, trying to catch Georgia's eye. "I don't think I should," she said.

"Tell us what?" Mikki demanded.

"You know all those posts on Stalkerazzi about Georgia doing this, Georgia wearing whatever she's wearing?" Nova said. "And all the cameraguys always knowing where to find her? How do you think that happens? She *makes* it happen."

"What are you saying?" Mikki said. "Georgia hates that."

"Oh, I doubt that very much," Nova said. "Sivya, tell them."

"It's true," Sivya burst out. "I found all the e-mails on her computer when I was fixing it. I'm sorry, Georgia. It just sort of slipped out, and I'm an awful liar."

Georgia looked as mortified as Elizabeth had felt in Ms. Bishop's office.

Nailah spoke up. "Georgia, so you really tell the

66 *Is there something wrong with your brain, Georgia?* **99**

paparazzi where to find you? That's . . . it's quite odd."

"It's disgusting," Mikki said.

"I think it's pathetic," Nova added. "All that stuff with that supposed bike messenger we saw you with on Stalkerazzi this morning . . . was that a setup, too? Does he even *exist*?"

"He's real," Georgia whispered. "I swear."

"See what I mean?" Nova said.

"Yeah, if Georgia didn't tell Ms. Bishop—"

"Then Elizabeth would have been sent home anyway," Asha said. She stepped into the middle of the room. "You don't think Ms. Bishop would have figured it out? And if she hadn't, if the story had been published? Elizabeth could have gotten *Flirt* sued. We're talking about *plagiarism* here. Who cares about Georgia's dumb obsession with getting into *Us Weekly*. I mean, really."

Elizabeth shrunk. Everyone's eyes were on her again.

Asha's right. What I did was so much worse.

"Elizabeth," Asha said, "why did you do it? I don't get it. I just don't understand why you would cheat rather than go to Ms. Bishop and ask for more time."

"Was it all the partying? Should I have left you alone

more?" Mikki said. She was really taking this hard, as if she'd had something to do with it.

"Why didn't you ask us for help?" Sivya asked.

Elizabeth couldn't take it anymore. "I don't know, okay? It was stupid. *I* was stupid. I made an awful mistake, girls. There's no excuse."

The buzzer rang. Someone was arriving on the elevator. It was a messenger, there to pick up something from Georgia. She quietly handed over a large envelope, signed a form, and the messenger was off.

"That wasn't *your* messenger, was it?" Mikki asked.

"No!" Georgia said.

"Didn't you see the photos?" Nova said. "Her messenger is much cuter. But what was that about, Georgia?"

"I turned down the part in the movie," Georgia announced. "The messenger was just picking up the script. I guess it's so confidential, they don't want me to hang onto it."

"You turned it down?" Sivya said. "That means you're staying?"

"Yeah, I'm staying," Georgia said with a glance at Elizabeth.

"You just turned down a Mirra movie," Nova said dully. "Is there something wrong with your brain, Georgia?"

Even Nailah looked floored about the news.

"I just really want to do this internship," Georgia said. "I've always wanted to write. That probably doesn't make sense to anyone, but—"

"I think it makes sense," Elizabeth said. "I understand, Georgia, really I do."

"Well, I think she's crazy," Nova said.

"I think she's the sanest person here," Elizabeth said. "I'd stay, too. If I could."

⊙　　⊙　　⊙　　⊙

It was Elizabeth's last night, but she didn't want to go to a party, or even out clubbing. She just wanted to hang out like it was any normal night, and so that's what they did: watching reruns of *Flirt It!*, eating popcorn, trying out Asha's latest hair-conditioning concoction and hoping it wouldn't turn their hair green, that kind of thing.

But in the middle of the night, Elizabeth woke and wandered into the hallway. There was a light on in the art studio. Inside, she found Mikki at her easel. She'd pasted photographs of the city parks onto a canvas and was painting on them. There was paint in her hair, paint on her cheek, paint on her smock, and a gob of paint flew across the room and spattered at Elizabeth's feet. That's when Mikki turned and found her standing there.

"Hi," Elizabeth said. The green paint had missed her toe by a few inches.

"Hey," Mikki said.

There was an awkward silence.

"So, do you think I'm disgusting?" Elizabeth asked.

"No!" Mikki said. Then she covered her mouth because she was being loud. "Close the door, mate," she said, "so we can talk."

"But you're in the middle of painting. You look really inspired."

Mikki glanced at her canvas—greens and blues and yellows amid the stark black-and-white of her photos. "I am."

"So am I," Elizabeth said. "I woke up with all these ideas, whole lines in my head." She rolled her eyes. "My own lines this time, not anybody else's."

"Get your laptop, then," Mikki said. "We'll be creative together."

Elizabeth went to grab her laptop and that's how she spent the rest of the night, there with Mikki, writing up a storm while Mikki painted. Sometimes they stopped in the middle of a sentence or a stroke of paint and talked about inspiration, and art, and the possibilities of the future, and the regrets of the past. Other times they worked silently, comfortably, side by side, the art they were creating the only thing they had to say.

What Elizabeth had by morning was a whole essay. It was about struggling to find your own voice. It was the most honest thing she'd written in a long time.

This is what I should have written, she thought.

Before she could talk herself out of it, she e-mailed it to Ms. Bishop. Really, she had nothing more to lose.

⟳   ⟳   ⟳   ⟳

The car was waiting for Elizabeth downstairs. They kept the farewells simple—everyone still seemed in shock—but Mikki shrugged off the good-bye hug and followed Elizabeth into the elevator and down to the curb. Once the suitcases were in the trunk, they stood on the sidewalk, unsure of what to say.

"You'll write me," Mikki said at last.

"Definitely," Elizabeth said. "And you have to keep in touch, too. You have to tell me what you do for the *Flirt It!* show. And tell me about every single club Nova takes you to. And if Asha turns anyone's lips funny colors again, you've got to call me. And Sivya, she's so cute. If you ever get her in a dress again, you have to send me pictures. And Nailah, I feel like I hardly got to know her! As for Georgia, I'm sure I'll hear *all* about her online." She grinned. "But Mikki, you've got to write me, too. Okay?"

"I don't write," Mikki said. "I don't write letters, don't do 'em. But I'll read yours, and I'll send you pictures, no doubt."

Then they heard the sound of a throat clearing. Georgia had come down, too. "Can I talk to you?" she said to Elizabeth.

Mikki stepped back. "I'm going up. I don't do the good-bye thing, either."

Elizabeth watched her go, and that was that. She'd made some incredible friends this summer. She'd met some amazing girls, and they made her want to be more of herself, whoever that was. She wouldn't give that up for the world.

"I came down to say I'm sorry," Georgia announced. "I mean, really."

Elizabeth almost laughed. But Georgia was standing there in her pajamas, her hair not yet blown dry from her shower—and she never left the loft without doing her hair, since the cameras were always on her. She wasn't even wearing sunglasses.

"It's okay, Georgia. I'm the one who messed up."

"But I shouldn't have ratted you out. And . . . especially now that I know you're writing your novel about me, I just, I feel awful. You must think I'm a monster."

"I don't, really."

"So, about your novel . . . do you know who you're dedicating it to yet?"

"I'll send you more chapters, once I write them, I promise, but—"

"But what?" Georgia said, her eyes narrowing. "Please tell me your character doesn't turn into a demented cheerleader or something."

"No, I have a lot of work to do on that. My agent—before we show publishers or anyone—she wants me to just finish it. Write what I'm gonna write, and take however long it takes. She doesn't think I'm ready for a book deal just yet."

"Oh," Georgia said. "Too bad. How long do you think it'll take?"

"Probably a long time."

"That's fine," Georgia said. "Just don't make me too much of a diva, okay?"

Elizabeth kept her lips sealed.

"So, what're you gonna do this summer now that, you know, you have nothing else to do?" Georgia asked.

Elizabeth shrugged. Quietly she said, "I have no idea."

"You could go to Mexico," Georgia shot out. Then she said, "I'm kidding. Sorry."

Elizabeth felt heat rise to her face. "I've always wanted to travel. I guess what I mean is I don't know what I'll do. It's all up in the air. And that's kind of . . . nice."

> **" Please tell me your character doesn't turn into a demented cheerleader or something. "**

Georgia nodded without judgment. "Totally."

"Listen, I have to go. My mom's waiting for me, and then—you know."

Georgia stepped forward and pulled Elizabeth into a hug. It was stiff, awkward, but it was the first time they'd hugged, or touched really. She didn't know what to say.

"See ya," Georgia said. Then she headed back into the building.

Elizabeth got into the car. From the window in the backseat, she craned her neck to see up to the top-floor windows of the interns' loft. The girls were in there, running around, getting ready for another day at the office.

How lucky they are, Elizabeth thought. *They get to stay.*

      ☉   ☉   ☉   ☉

From: melwrites247@freemail.com
To: elizabeth_cheekwood@webdotmail.com
Re: CONGRATS!

Lizzy,

I just heard through the grapevine (okay, I made friends with the copy editor. A piece of advice: always make friends with the copy editor) that your essay's in the next issue! I can't wait to read it. The copy editor said there's some big news about you, but he had a deadline and said he'd tell me later. So what's your big news? Tell! I just tried your FLIRT e-mail address, but you know what's weird? My message got returned "Recipient Unknown" or whatever. You should talk to the tech people and get that fixed. It's like, hello?, the magazine thinks you no longer work there!

Congrats again!
—Melanie Henderson
former Features intern

ⓖ   ⓖ   ⓖ   ⓖ

stalkerazzi.com

Currently stalking . . . oh, you know we can't stop ourselves from spying on Georgia Cooper, especially after she's seen with that mystery guy—we've all seen the pictures. (Georgia: Why aren't you answering our e-mails? Don't you love us anymore?)

But the hottie on the bike isn't our only Georgia news. Are you sitting down, faithful stalkers? Rumor has it that Georgia was offered a feature role in a Very Hot movie and—get this—she turned it down to keep her lowly intern gig at *Flirt*. Is there something in the water over at the Hudson-

Bennett building? Take our poll below and help us figure out what's going on. We're stumped.

Why oh why did Georgia Cooper turn down the movie role of a lifetime?

(a) She wanted to take the role, but she's been imprisoned by Jonah Jones in *Flirt's* Fashion Closet and no one can find her behind all the Chanel.

(b) She's under a sinister form of hypnosis. If Jo Bishop claps twice, Georgia spit-shines her Manolos. If Jo claps three times, Georgia quacks like a duck.

(c) She's discovered her true calling in life: fetching lattes and making photocopies. Who needs the Meisner technique once you learn how to collate?

(d) She's fallen hard for a bicycle messenger and refuses to leave New York. (Actually, that might be true.)

(e) Hey, give her a break. She just wants to try something new.

VOTE NOW!